THE WOMAN W[...]
TO HER[...]

A. L. Barker left school w[...] after the War, joined the BBC. Her [...] of short stories, *Innocents*, won the first-e[...] Somerset Maugham Prize in 1947, and her novel, *John Brown's Body*, was shortlisted for the Booker McConnell Prize in 1969. She is the author of nine novels, most recently, *The Gooseboy*, hailed by Philip Howard in *The Times* as 'a delightful novel... A. L. Barker has a strong idiosyncrasy and a sharp eye for precise detail. She has original and entertaining notions about everything', and seven short story collections, including the autobiographical *Life Stories*.

A. L. Barker lives in Surrey.

BY THE SAME AUTHOR

Novels
Apology for a Hero
A Case Examined
The Middling
John Brown's Body
A Source of Embarrassment
A Heavy Feather
Relative Successes
The Gooseboy

Stories
Innocents
Novelette
The Joy Ride and After
Lost Upon the Roundabouts
Femina Real
Life Stories
No Word of Love

'The tenth novel by A. L. Barker, *The Woman Who Talked to Herself*, is technically a *tour de force*. Her voice is as idiosyncratic as ever: sharp and condensed, often demanding, even cavalier with the reader; her style breathless with asyndeton, startling tense changes, shifts of gear, and sudden, penetrating witticisms. The narrator is a middle-aged storyteller, Winnie Appleton, and the narrative lynchpin is the interview she is giving a young journalist, Angie. The bulk of the book, however, is a handful of apparently unconnected short stories, all finely wrought, some left tantalisingly in the air... each little world is brilliantly realised'
Daily Telegraph

'This new book by A. L. Barker is ceaselessly entertaining and brimming with acute insights into a multiplicity of lives and characters. Described by the authoress as an "articulated novel" it combines the genres of novel and short story (Barker has published nearly as many volumes of stories as novels) to produce a sparklingly inventive hybrid. Ostensibly a recollection by professional story-teller, Winifred Appleton, who has achieved the unlikely feat for a fiction-pedlar of packing out Wembley Stadium, the narrative is diversified through a series of fantasies provoked by incidents from Winifred's life. A chance meeting or chance mention will turn her prismatic mind to new stories, many of which are self-contained vignettes of dazzling originality'
Literary Review

'The stories read like daydreams from which we awaken to the often painful and abrupt denouement. They are Winnie's fantasies, her way of controlling and transforming the disappointments and anxieties in her own life: her husband's infidelity, her son's efforts to break free of his parents, her daughter's infatuation with another mother. This is why she distrusts the written word, for like her family it can change, can be treacherous. These extraordinary stories, grotesque, compassionate, unpredictable, are deftly written. Barker has written a highly original work which is as much about the creation of fiction, its roots in the author's fears and desires, its accretion of detail, as it is about the failure of dream to match reality'
Financial Times

'Barker is a wholly original writer, and one now totally in command of the craft which she has been practising with so much distinction for more than 40 years. That she is not better known to the public at large, as distinct from her admiring fellow writers, has always been a puzzle to me'
Spectator

A. L. Barker

The Woman Who Talked to Herself

An Articulated Novel

VINTAGE

VINTAGE

20 Vauxhall Bridge Road, London SW1V 2SA

London Melbourne Sydney Auckland Johannesburg
and agencies throughout the world

First published by Hutchinson, 1989
Vintage edition 1991

© A. L. Barker 1989

The right of A. L. Barker to be identified as the author of this work has been asserted by her in accordance with the Copyright, Designs and Patents Act, 1988

This book is sold subject to the condition that it shall not, by way of trade or otherwise, be lent, resold, hired out, or otherwise circulated without the publisher's prior consent in any form of binding or cover other than that in which it is published and without a similar condition including this condition being imposed on the subsequent purchaser

Printed and bound in Great Britain by
Cox & Wyman Ltd, Reading

ISBN 0 09 970440 4

The Woman Who Talked to Herself

An articulated novel

OUR CAT, HOVIS, is asleep on the rush-bottomed chair. As she sits down she feels his animal warmth, and she blushes.

She has surprised me in the kitchen making a steak and kidney pie, expressing myself through my pastry. She wants to talk about my art. I tell her it's more of a bodily function.

Her editor said go and talk to that woman who makes a career telling stories, the one who filled Wembley Stadium, Winnie Appleton, with a talent to amuse. (You could also learn, listening to me.)

'I never thought what I do would interest the media.'

She says I am a success in an unexplored sphere.

'You mean like one of the rings of Saturn? Dickens was before me.'

She reminds me that Dickens was before the electronic era, he had no competition from radio and television. She has heard that other people are trying to do what I do, they are telling stories in pubs and halls all over the country.

My success is due to my persona. My stories *are* my persona and I don't mind what other people do because their personas are nothing like mine.

But she wants to know why I do it, it's the question her editor will ask.

My pastry is sticking to the rolling-pin, it is full of holes and stretchy like an old vest. 'As a child I was unable to read. I screamed when they tried to teach me. I don't like the look of words. They're so arbitrary.'

She says we have to identify.

'I prefer the element of doubt.'

She can see that I might, but knows that her editor will require identification. I ball up my pastry, sprinkle flour and re-roll it. She is young and pretty, I have seen her modelling for shampoos and dinner-mints.

'I didn't catch your name.'

'Call me Angie.'

'And the name of your magazine?'

'We'll send you a contract before we use anything. So there'll be no mistake.'

'Any mistake will be mine.'

'Why do you dislike words?'

'I said I don't like the look of them. It's not the same thing.'

'Is arbitrariness your only reason?'

'No.'

'Are you going to tell me?' Careless of her nice elbows she props them in the flour, holding her chin in her hands, a child waiting for the bedtime story.

With the pastry scraps I fashion a Tudor rose for the top of my pie. When it comes out of the oven the rose will have softened and shrunk and no one will know it was a rose.

What shall I tell her? It must be clear cut and definitive.

'I'm glad you're here, you'll help me through this chore.'

'Do you find cooking boring?'

'Dead boring. Necro-buggery.' She thinks that I shouldn't know about such things. 'It was a graffito I liked.'

'So you didn't mind those words?'

'It's the printed page I don't like.' She has started to mistrust me, she sees her piece being invalidated. 'My aversion dates back to the day Father Christmas went on fire. I suffered from alexia.'

She removes her elbows from my pastry-board and looks about her. She thinks truth is the real thing and only wants seeing.

I tap the pudding basin with my knife, like a conductor silencing an orchestra. 'I'm going to tell you. When I was very small, my parents didn't get on, and they often talked about why. They looked over my head when they talked and it made me think I wasn't tall enough to be spoken to. I climbed on a chair, thinking to reach them, and my father put me out of the room. What do you do when you're not tall enough? You must wait until you are. But by the time I was, they weren't talking at all. My father had gone and my mother had married Father Christmas.'

At this point I should give her something solid for her piece. I begin: 'It was the night before Christmas. I was four years old and I had been told that Father Christmas would come down the chimney to see me.

'We had a gas fire that burned blue and orange and made popping noises. When Father Christmas came he wore a baggy red blouse like one of my mother's. It reassured me, as did his cotton-wool beard which was nothing like real. His legs were reassuring too, because he wore dark blue trousers with a red stripe like the man who often came to see my mother and who worked on the buses. I had no trouble associating big red buses with Father Christmas: to my way of thinking they were more suitable than reindeer for getting him and his parcels about.

'When he took me on his knee he smelled like the man from the buses. There we were, Father Christmas, my mother and me, and the gas fire popping. He had brought me a storybook with pictures in it. I pushed my finger over them, pointed out and named what I saw: Pussy, Bow-wow, Moo-cow, Gee-gee, putting them into spoken words. I hadn't started to learn to read, and print meant nothing to me.

'My mother, a hasty woman, tried to hurry us. Santa of the buses was patient and we sat for a long time over the pictures. Mother grew restless, she whispered in his ear and pulled his whiskers. He turned a page and began to read. He had a nice voice, soft and lazy. It soothed Mother, and as for me, I was witnessing a miracle coming out of his whiskers. I thought his whiskers instrumental, it wouldn't be too much to say I thought they were the instrument. Two strips of grubby cotton wool!'

'Children have such vivid imaginations.'

'Imagination nothing, it was logic, and bang on as it happened.

'That was a perfect time. Complete. Even young children have reservations but I didn't feel them then, and I don't now. I can pick that time up and it's still a perfect whole. I wasn't wanting anything more, sitting in Father Christmas's lap I watched the black hooks and eyes on the page come out of his wool whiskers as words. Such lovely words: "Snow White and the Seven Dwarfs", "Once upon a time . . ." It was the whole of life.

'My mother put her arms around Father Christmas and kissed his cheek, thanking him for the words—and for something else, I daresay. We were halfway through Snow White when my father walked in.

'I never did hear the end of that story. Do you know it?'

'Well, yes—'

'What happened to the wolf?'

'The wolf was in something else.'

'My father coming in like that broke the moment, though it couldn't have lasted much longer the way my mother was carrying on, nuzzling and biting Father Christmas.'

Angie waits. She has made no notes, as yet there has been no reversion of the spoken word to written. But I suppose it would be called a progression.

'My father came into the room, my mother screamed and my father struck a match on his thumbnail—it was his party-trick—and held the flame to Santa's beard.'

'Oh dear.'

'You could say that. My father went away and left my mother and me without any money. Santa Claus turned out to be the man from the buses. He was badly burned and the buses wouldn't have him back when he came out of hospital for fear he would frighten the passengers. Our sofa smouldered for days.

'Do you see what I mean about words being arbitrary? I can look back at that Christmas Eve and it's dear, it's precious. I look again and it's dear because it cost us. I can't trust a word that means plus one minute and minus the next. I'll tell you something else. That same word can mean plus and minus at the same time. If you hold something dear it will cost you dear.'

'I didn't come to discuss semantics.'

'You came to find out why I tell stories. This is why: the book went on fire. The pages turned brown and the print shrivelled up and I wanted never to look at another word.'

'But you have looked.'

'I can't avoid it. We're smothered in print. A million trees a minute are cut down for paper. It can't go on, we shall have to telemit, communicate with each other through the airwaves.'

'Is it true that you filled Wembley Stadium?'

'I believe there were a few seats left in the top back rows. The amplifiers distorted my voice, so I told a distorted story.'

She soldiers on. 'Thousands of people come to listen to you. If you were to appear on television you could command even bigger audiences.'

'But third parties—technicians—would get between me and my audience. Direct communication, person to person, is the art of storytelling.'

'We shall want pictures to go with the article. A big picture of you.'

'It will have to be big.' Angie is slight and wandish, she could be made of wicker. Wicker bones, straw veins. I ask if she is writing a book.

'Oh no, I couldn't.'

'Everyone can, everyone is. Except me. Will it be an autobiography?'

'I couldn't write about myself.'

I tell her that journalism is no profession for receptacles, least of all baskets. Ovens, yes, an oven is necessary because there's cooking up to be done.

Staring at yourself in the mirror is a sure way of picking up a germ. I picked up a germ of fear. I feared I didn't exist. I was sleeping and waking, but not being. My children went to school, my husband went to work. I was left in the house, as was the dust, and the egg on the plates. But the dust had settled and the egg had nourished.

My husband said, 'Think we should get the house painted?' and I said, 'Next year will be soon enough,' and he rang the builder and asked him to start. I knitted a football jersey for my son and he said, 'You've got the colours wrong, it's red over green, not green over red.' I said, 'I'll unrip it and do it again.' He said, 'Just buy one. OK?' In the supermarket people bumped me with trolleys and apologised to the chicken thighs. People spoke, nobody talked.

I blame my mother for making me solitary. She was sexually aware, and took all her chances. She wasn't above making them. I knew from babyhood that sex was something which wouldn't wait. I saw it coming in the way she lifted her arm, turned her head, walked along the street. I knew when it was coming, I didn't know what it was, it just came between her and me. I stopped trying to get close after she married Father Christmas. She had no time for me. When I say time I don't mean hours and minutes, she gave me enough of those to keep me clean and fed. I mean contemporaneity.

I tried to get into her world, to see what she saw and feel what she felt. I laugh about it now: myself, diligent child, following her, dogging her, trying, God help me, to feel the joys and expectations of sex. What a drag I must have been. And she let me know it. She shut doors in my face, shooed me like a chicken.

I was lonely. After Father Christmas lost his job on the buses he went to work as a labourer and we lived in a tied cottage in the middle of a heath. There were no children for me to be with and I was too young to make the journey to school.

I didn't have a dolls' house. I made houses in the furze. It takes willpower to believe you're having domestic and social encounters in thorn bushes. I had to stretch my imagination and I've never been able to get it back to normal. Whatever normal is.

Ross and Mayhew, friends of my son Maurice, have been caught trying to break into one of the big normal houses in Palmyra Road, built for Victorian gentlefolk, Queen and Empire in every brick, coopy attics for the servants, iron-framed crystal palaces for the plants.

The householder caught the boys. He laughed about it, said there was no harm done, they couldn't possibly have forced an entry. They aren't grateful, they feel they've been made to look foolish. Ross declares he could have got through the upstairs lavatory window, he calls himself Snakehips. Maurice says he's a bad influence on Mayhew. Mayhew's flabby, he says. He disapproves of them.

I

A CAR WITH luggage on the roof drove out of the gate and Ross nudged Mayhew, the thought in both their minds. They went round after dark and there were no lights in the house. Ross spotted a small window at the back which was not quite closed.

Mayhew said, 'You'll never get through that.'

Ross boasted he could get through the overflow pipe if need be. 'Find me a ladder.'

'Where?'

'How do I know?'

Actually that part was easy. They found a ladder on the wall of the garage, the back door of which was locked. Mayhew went straight to a loose flagstone, under it was the key. Ross said, 'People deserve to be ripped off.'

Mayhew said, 'We're not going to rip them off.'

Ross can pass for a twelve-year-old, though he is in mid-teens, slender, would be dark-haired but his head is shaved. He has a sweet-natured mouth and a milky skin, skimmed over his cheekbones.

Mayhew likes to be called 'Ape'. He has made a hairy start and wears his jeans repressively tight to show that he cannot be repressed. 'Let's go in soon.'

'With all the gear they took, they'll be away for weeks.'

'What if they were just taking it to the tip?'

'I like an element of risk.'

Mayhew locked the garage and put the key under the stone. He likes to be ahead and will take every precaution against being left behind. 'We'll check it out tomorrow night.'

'Not me. I've got a date.'

'I may go in.'

Ross laughed. 'You couldn't.'

He is quite sure. Mayhew would give anything to be able to carry off surety with Ross's easy conscience. 'Who says I couldn't?'

'You're not built for it, I am. Snakehips!'

Ross has snake's eyes, speckled gold, and shallow. It is not possible to see into them. He makes Mayhew feel stupid. But if he is right, he can also be wrong. Mayhew doubts if anyone could get through that window. A skinny kid of six, perhaps. Ross is the size of a skinny kid twice that age. Mayhew expects to have fun watching.

What he had, the night they went in, a bad wet night, was rain down his neck, and a lot of worry. He stood below watching Ross, and could feel himself getting sensible and asking why were they doing this. Ross had one leg through the window and the major part of his backside.

Ross started singing. Mayhew, alarmed, hissed at him to shut up. Ross gave the window a bash, but it was open as far as it would go. He withdrew his leg and, standing on the ladder, put his head and one shoulder through. His feet slipped, the ladder lurched.

Mayhew just managed to hold it. 'Pack it in!'

'I'm trying. I never said it would be easy.'

Ross, who had said just that, stepped off the ladder onto the sill. Using a handhold on a pipe-neck projecting above the window, he drove both feet through the aperture and finished with his legs in and his thighs out. 'How can I do this?'

'You can't!'

'I can, because the window's not square. It's taller than it's wide, so I go in at an angle.' He whistled through his teeth, a man doing a tricky job. 'I may take my pants off.'

'Why?'

'If an angle of forty-five degrees isn't enough I'll have to grease myself. Find me some motor oil.' Mayhew could feel his cool getting warm. Something dropped on his head, something soft, with arms. Ross had thrown off his anorak. 'It's going to be more than forty-five.'

15

Mayhew swore aloud, then fretted about being overheard.

'I've got to be scientific.' Ross turned on his side, clinging by one hand to the downpipe. Bits of concrete rained down. 'I'm stuck.'

'Snakehips!'

'My potential's stopping me. It's big between the legs.'

'Put it through a bit at a time.'

Ross peered under his armpit. 'Some things are a sacred trust. I owe it to posterity. Come up and give me a shove.'

Mayhew climbed the ladder. When he was on the top rung, behind Ross, he looked up at the roof. It was as if someone had kicked him in the knees. He swayed and the ladder jerked away from the wall.

'Stop fooling about. Put your hands on my back and push.'

'You'll never do it.'

'My arse is a single unit but I can put my shoulders through one at a time. Don't cling, man—push!'

Mayhew pushed, using brute force. It was better to be brutish than sick, which was the next feeling he was about to have. Ross sank in past his waist. Mayhew left him making swimming motions with his arms and went back down the ladder. On the ground he started to retch. When next he looked up at the window Ross had disappeared.

Ross admitted him by the front door, into a big hall. It was semi-dark. Mayhew could make out bearskin rugs, leather chairs, a copper-hooded fireplace, horsebrasses, a staircase that could be marble.

'Nice!'

'Not bad.' Ross spoke as if he owned it, standing with his jeans screwed up over his calves. He could be ridiculous, just as part of being himself. 'Did you bring a light?'

'You've got the torch.'

'In my anorak pocket. Get it.'

'You want it, you get it.'

Ross started up the stairs, whistling. Mayhew had to go for the anorak which was still lying outside under the ladder. When he got back to the hall, Ross was nowhere to be seen. Mayhew called softly. For answer he heard shushing rain and the steady trudge of a clock, a grandfather by the sound.

He relied a lot on his sense of smell. It was a form of direct contact with the people who had gone away. Sometimes he could tell what they had had for dinner before they went. He tried to decide if they were the sort of people he could have got on with. He and Ross have been into quite a few houses. They went out of idle curiosity at first, but that crystallised into a principle. Participation. They had the right. It is non-covetous on Mayhew's part, he simply likes to know what he is missing. Ross simply is not going to be left out.

Here was Mayhew now, smelling deep old leather, fusty old bearskins and the reek of the wet ivy which grew over the front of the house. He groped along a passage, his eyes suiting themselves to the degree of dark. When he opened a door it was obvious that he had come to the kitchen. There was a lot of stripped pine and banks of domestic appliances. The freezer dial made a green twilight.

On the dresser was a memo pad and pencil. Mayhew drew a circle, put in eyes, nose and a rake of teeth and wrote 'Hallo!' underneath. It was probably the most definitive thing he would do.

Other people's possessions do not tempt him, taking them doesn't make them his. It is not morality, just that he has private means which he expects to come into any day, and meantime keeps himself to himself, avoids getting mixed up or rubbed off or stuck with other people.

Ross is no sticker, he is solo, and slippery with it. He has nothing Mayhew wants, except confidence, which he misuses. When Mayhew comes into his own he will know what to do with it.

Back in the hall he suddenly measured his length. He had stumbled over the glass-eyed snarling head of a bear. He touched the arched tongue, it was hard as iron.

A door slammed overhead, Ross's whistle cut down the dark. 'Bring a light.' He was at the top of the stairs, holding something to his chest.

'What's that?'

'It has to be them, on their wedding-day. Shine the torch.' The framed photograph showed a couple in a church doorway, the bearded man wearing a morning suit, in the act of raising his top hat, and at his side a young prettyish woman in bridal white, dripping with carnations. 'Look at the hairy woubit. One of the chosen.'

'How do you know?'

'He's grinning like he just blew down Jericho.'

'He just got married.'

'He looks like you.'

'He's bald!'

'So will you be. You'll lose your hair before you're thirty.'

'I will not!'

'I bet she wanted something better than him.' Ross ran his finger over the woman. 'I hope she's getting it. Money's not everything, a woman needs sexual fulfillment as much as a man. You wouldn't know, you're macho, no imagination.'

'You know what you are?' Unwise of Mayhew to ask, because Ross is something special. 'You're a—' He waited openmouthed for it to come to him. When it didn't, he supplied the old word. 'Shit.'

'Sure.'

'Dog shit!'

Ross pushed open a door. 'This is their bedroom.'

'And?'

'So take a look.'

Mayhew didn't care for the way Ross stood aside, as if he had something lined up. He went in warily, pooling the torch beam at his feet.

There was light enough from the street lamp outside for him to see the room and get a surprise. Wherever he looked there were depths, it was more like a bubble than a room. He saw watery shapes, more like fish, flying in the depths. He swung round.

Ross was waving his arms. 'It's all done with mirrors. See? The hairy woubit likes to watch himself perform.'

'Nice bed.' Mayhew lay down on it. Ross leaped over him, landing feet first. They bounced together, Ross standing, and Mayhew on his back, laughing, until he looked up and saw the mirror in the ceiling. He rolled off the bed. A strong sweetish perfume from the satin spread got up his nose. 'Is there anything to eat?'

Ross, who had been swiping at the overhead mirror, gave a bound as if on a trampoline and executed a partial somersault ending in a belly-flop. 'Look here.' He slid back the door of a built-in wardrobe.

'Old clothes.'

'I can tell people by what they wear. Her, for instance, she's a tart-mankey.'

'What?'

'Mankey's French for you'd like to be but you're not.'

Mayhew never knew how much to believe. 'How do you know?'

'I took French lessons, I thought of going as an au-pair.'

'How do you know about her?'

'Split skirts, plunge necklines. This—' Ross pulled out a pink and white thing, all ribbon bows and lace—'all wasted on the woubit.' Mayhew found a bowler hat and clapped it on. They laughed. Ross was first to stop. 'If he's chosen, what does that make us?'

Mayhew recognised one of Ross's spurts of rage. They are shortlived and quirky. If Jews think they can get ahead wearing funny caps and not eating pork, that is their business. Mayhew doesn't give a hoot for the kind of thing that rattles Ross. 'I'll go look in the fridge.'

'It makes us slag. Because of what was written on some old stones two thousand years ago. It's never been proved what was on them. If anything was. How's that for a con?'

'Think there'll be sausages?'

'Hitler went to a lot of trouble because he wasn't chosen and couldn't stand being second-bananas. He could have saved himself all those progroms and used the manpower to fight the war. He might have won.'

'They don't have to be pork sausages.'

'Here's something else. What do you know!' Ross hauled out a military jacket from the depths of the wardrobe. 'He's a soldier!'

'So?'

'Captain—no, he's Major Woubit. Look at his flashes. And a service stripe. It's all here.' Ross dived into the cupboard. 'Britches, boots, belt. You'd look good in these. It's your style. I see you as an army man.'

'Get away.'

'No, straight up, I mean it. I'd like to see you in uniform.' Ross threw the jacket at him. 'Put it on.'

'Why should I?'

'Go on, knock us cold.'

The coat weighed heavy in Mayhew's hands, felt important, nobody could deny its importance. When I say jump, you jump. He slipped it on, buttoned the crested brass.

'Now the britches.'

They were too big, so Mayhew pulled them over his jeans. Ross found a tie to secure the waist. Mayhew laced the breeches and pulled on the boots. Ross handed him the broad leather belt. Mayhew buckled it tight. 'Here's the cap and a swizzle stick. Man, you look great!'

Mayhew saw himself in the mirror, angled the peaked cap over one eye.

Ross clapped him on the shoulder. 'You should join the army, get a commission and watch the women fall over. That uniform does it all.'

Mayhew pointed the cane at him. 'Attenshun!'

'Yessir!'

'About turn, forward march!'

He had Ross marching, marking time, shouldering arms, bawled him out for being improperly dressed, flicked up Ross's T-shirt on the end of his cane, and Ross played along, acting the tenderfoot, the conscript still wet behind the ears. When I say die, you die.

They climbed on the bed, pretended it was a tank and Ross acted gun-turret. Mayhew spun him round, sighting along his outstretched arm, firing.

Mayhew caught glimpses of himself in the mirrors. There wasn't enough light to see detail, but he looked fine, he looked Someone. General Mayhew CO of the Expeditionary Forces. It was a happy time. He wanted nothing more, not even reality. Especially not reality.

Then Ross broke it up. 'What about that nosh? I'm starving.'

'You always bloody are. What'll you do when the world supply of food runs out?'

'Eat people. Cooked right they're very nice. Go and see what there is.'

'I'm not in the catering corps. I'm a General.'

Mayhew found he was having difficulty with the uniform. He felt clobbered. The breeches dragged at his thighs, the tunic weighed on him and the cap smelled hairy. He ran downstairs, smacking the boots with the cane.

The fridge was empty but the chest freezer was packed, the stuff covered with ice and iron-hard. He could have knocked someone out with one of the shoulders of lamb. While he was leaning over to identify the food the cap fell off his head. He dug out a packet of fish-fingers, a pizza, a stick loaf and a Black Forest gateau and left the hat in the freezer.

The microwave was no problem, there is one at home and he is accustomed to fixing meals for himself. He defrosted the food and put in the pizza and the fish to reheat. While he waited, he ate a slice of gateau.

When the food was ready he whistled up the stairs. He was damned if he was going to wait on Ross. Sitting on the bottom step he ate the pizza and mopped up with bread.

There was still the gateau. He has a weakness for dark chocolate, but suddenly he was conscious of the house, the set-up and his place in it. Something was owing to the uniform and it wasn't just cake.

In a room off the hall he found the drinks. He poured whisky and took a sip. He has to conceal, now and for ever, the fact that he doesn't like the taste of spirits. He likes dark chocolate.

A click and he was in a blaze, shocked out of his wits. The light had been switched on. He'd been discovered, the woman in the doorway was the wife returned.

She was young and trendy, as Ross had said she would be, wore scarlet knee-pants, a gold-thread top that left her shoulders bare, a turban tied in a mammy-knot, earrings, necklaces, platform shoes. She stood propped in the doorway, slowly sliding one arm up the frame and leaning on it. Bangles slid, jingling, from her wrist to her armpit. She had thin arms, very white. Her breasts bothered Mayhew: they had points, the usual ones, and others—as if they were prickly.

He still held the whisky glass, whisky still in it. He thought of throwing it in her face and making a run. But she came towards him, smiling, and he remembered Ross saying about her wanting to be a tart. She had a tart's face, green eyeshadow and a glistening red mouth. She looked into his eyes, hers were light, shallow eyes, speckled gold. Mayhew's heart knocked on his ribs.

'Cool it,' she said. Mayhew's heart stopped beating. He felt himself swelling fit to burst. 'Don't I look something?'

Mayhew, who should have exploded, let out a whimper. 'You look like a tart!'

'Fantastico.'

'You crazy? Switching on the light—'

'You have to see me.'

'I should kill you!'

Ross lifted his loaded eyelashes on his fingers. 'I can't get these falsies right. It's like wearing a drawbridge. Help me take them off.'

Mayhew dived for the switch and shut off the light.
'The cops will be here directly—'

'Stop griping and be fun.'

'Fun!'

'You're not the only one who likes to dress up.'

'You should see yourself, you should take a good look.'

'I did, and I look good. I like looking good. So do you. You in your way, me in mine.'

'Your way's screwy.'

Ross was stretching himself, lazily. The bangles jingled. 'I'll get myself some nice things. Frocks, a panty-belt in black lace, a blonde wig. I couldn't find Mrs Woubit's foam-cups, I had to pad myself with paper hankies. Haven't got them right, have I?'

So far as Mayhew could tell, he was serious. The trouble is Mayhew can never go far enough, with Ross it is never possible to be sure. Even in broad daylight, Mayhew can look into Ross's eyes and get nowhere. Ross is crazy like a fox.

'I like women's clothes. I like wearing them.'

'Har, har.'

'I like being a woman.'

In the hope of making the penny drop, Mayhew started a series of louder 'Hars'. They died in his throat as Ross came close.

'Could you fancy me?' His breath was moist on Mayhew's cheek. He walked two fingers up Mayhew's chest.

Mayhew's right leg reacted first. It came up, kneeing Ross in the groin. Ross howled and struck back. They fought, Mayhew ripped the off-the-shoulder blouse clean off him. Ross managed to get purchase, but nothing else, on the tabs of the uniform jacket.

Mayhew was determined to make Ross pay for his fun, for all the codding and conning he had done today and every other day. He threw Ross face down, got his knee in the small of Ross's back and did a thorough job working Ross's face into the floor, scrubbing off the make-up.

But Ross had something that served him better than muscle. He slid out of Mayhew's grip like a piece of wet soap and bounded to the other side of the room. He switched on the light. Mayhew, his mouth open, crouched on the floor, blinking.

Ross can diminish Mayhew with no justification. He did then, standing there with a brassière skewed across his naked chest, lipstick smeared over his jaw like jam.

Mayhew clambered to his feet, slowly, as if he was tired. He was itching to get Ross and the idea was to take him by surprise. 'Put that light out.'

'Darkness is the friend of criminals. I read that in our Neighbourhood Watchletter. So let there be light!' Ross opened wide his arms. Mayhew made as if to run into them, but before he could get near, Ross had whipped round and was dancing away. A swipe of his hand knocked on the switches in the hall. Mayhew had a glimpse like a nerve-flash of scarlet legs and a deeply-cleft butt springing up the stairs. On the landing Ross threw more switches. The house blazed, lighting up Mayhew like a goldfish in a goldfish bowl.

He went after Ross. It was not the smartest move, but he was ready—more than—to do him. God knew Ross was asking to be done.

The lights were on in the bedroom, multiplied and magnified by the mirrors. The only area of darkness was under the bed. Mayhew could have screamed: that, and a brass band, was all that was needed. It was too late to kill the lights, but there was Ross. Ross had always been there, and Mayhew was ready. He fixed Ross against one of the mirrors. He only had to push him through it.

Ross said 'Wait!' not as if he was scared, 'No, wait—' as if he would help Mayhew do it. 'Let me find something nice, something to turn you on. Wouldn't you like to see me in a see-through nightie?' If Mayhew could have believed, even the worst, he wouldn't have been desperate. It was not knowing, being dangled, made a fool of. 'You look lovely in that uniform.' Something cracked, the casing that keeps Mayhew together. He fell apart inside. 'Man, we could have fun!' Ross bared his teeth and poked the tip of his tongue between them.

Mayhew acted without further consideration. He pushed Ross into the wardrobe and dragged the door shut. Consideration was unnecessary because the door turned out to be flush-fitting and easy-rolling and it engaged with a strong spring lock at the end of its groove. Mayhew, who never trusted his luck, waited to see if it was operable from inside. He heard Ross wrenching at it, then start pounding.

Mayhew called out, 'I'm putting you in the cooler on a charge of failing to salute a superior officer.'

'Did anyone ever tell you what a load of fun you're not?'

'The sentence is a month's solitary.'

'Let me out before I kick this thing down.'

'Go ahead.'

Ross could be heard trying. But this was no fibreboard, self-assembly job, it was built into the wall. The front was solid oak to support the plate-glass mirrors.

'Christ, I think I've broken my toe.'

Mayhew stripped off the uniform. He felt dirty where it had touched him. Something he hadn't known about Ross was that he had a low pain threshold.

'Man, I'm in agony here!'

Mayhew threw the boots at the wardrobe. Then he went across the room and slammed the door.

Ross yelled until his voice cracked. Mayhew waited, standing inside the room. He listened with a sense of privilege, as the moments passed it began to sound less like Ross and more like a trapped rabbit.

'Cool it,' he said under his breath. He switched off the lights and let himself out. On the way downstairs he killed the other lights, put the house back into darkness.

He banged the front door as he went out. That was for Ross's benefit: nobody else would be listening. For once he was confident.

He didn't forget the ladder propped against the back wall of the house. He carried it into the garage, which he locked, replacing the key under the flagstone. There was just the small upstairs window still left open. Only Ross could get through that.

★

I have never shut my daughter out. She doesn't have to try to come into my world, I share hers. She has friends of her own age, I'm her playmate. Who better, knowing her as I do?

She has advantages I never had. She is too young to appreciate them, perhaps she never will. It's hard to be grateful for what you've always had.

My daughter, Melissa, has a dolls' house given her by her Granny Appleton. It is a scale model of the old manor where Granny Appleton was born and lived as a girl. It has barley-twist chimneys, casement windows and a prospect-room. The real house was pulled down years ago to make way for a leisure park, but Granny A has total recall and was able to instruct a carpenter to re-create it in miniature.

She talks about the manor as if it was a stately home. 'At The Manor Mr Lipscombe was head gardener and his word was law. He wouldn't have any but Cumberland stone for the paths.'

I've tried to like my mother-in-law. Arthur took me to the manor once, just before it was bulldozed, and I distinctly saw Granny Appleton in the garden, a little girl with golden curls paddling in the lily-pond. She turned and smiled at me, and I loved her. Afterwards I told her what I had seen and she said sharply, "There was never a lily-pond at the Manor. My father wanted one below the south terrace. Mr Lipscombe refused point-blank to dig up the lawn. And he was right. Looking from the prospect-room a pool would have interrupted the line of the garden.' When I asked her what a prospect-room was, she said, 'A room with a view of course'.

Although I'm not able to love her, I love her dolls' house. I unlatch the front and open it up. There are the rooms, cut down to size. Melissa sweeps them out with a pastry-brush, huffs on and rubs up the furniture, spit-washes the windows.

I tell her there's plenty of time for that, there'll be the time when she can't be anything but a housewife, the time when there's a shell of bricks and mortar on her back which she will have to carry around with her. At her age she should be having fun.

The dolls' house dolls are solid wood. Some stand, some sit, none of them can do both. Granny A didn't miniaturise the actual people who lived at the manor. Naturally not, they were mostly her own family. I remember Melissa picking up a man-doll and asking, 'Who's this?' and Granny A said 'We don't know anyone who keeps his hat on indoors.'

She doesn't suspect that when she cut her ancestral home down to size and gave it to Melissa, she did me a favour. She's a terrible snob and this plywood dummy is all she has left.

I have shared Melissa's life from the day she was born. Before that she shared mine. Carried under my heart, she was my conscience, moved me to laughter and tears, kicked me when I was down and when I was getting above myself. She had no pity and nothing was left to chance. Carrying her was the happiest time of my life.

It wasn't like that with Maurice. With him I felt the ordinary physical discomfort and onerousness of having a burden in my stomach. I was set on having a daughter. Maurice was like the train in the station, until he was out of the way there couldn't be another. I had to wait ten years.

At last Melissa came. I enter into her separate existence, the access points are the same as my own, only the territory is different. People don't understand our relationship. Granny Appleton tells me I'm at a difficult age. I expect that from her, but not from my husband. Once when Melissa and I were talking together he suddenly burst out 'For God's sake!' It really shook me. But I understood. He has a worrying job, he comes home for peace and relaxation and we are arguing about the rules of a skipping game. 'I'm sorry, I know you're tired,' I said. He sighed and gave me a little push. 'Leave the kid alone, eh?'

I might have told him what happens to a child left alone. I might have told him that when someone says half a word to such a child it has to make do for all the words that don't get spoken. I was such a child when the knife-grinder came and took our carving-knife and struck sparks from it on his wheel. To my mother he said, 'Now it will cut bacon wafers.' To me he said, 'Did you know pigs can see the wind?' and since then I've seen the wind as a knife with a brass handle like our old carver. I've given up telling my husband things like that. I know that if I do, he will think I'm trying to be noticed.

The view from the dolls' prospect-room is of Melissa's wellies. The house is in her bedroom, we sit on the floor to act our happenings. We make up people for the dolls. Each doll has to be several people because there are not enough dolls for all the parts. Some of them are darker than the others because Melissa once buried them in the garden. She kept them hidden for a week, then I found them and dug them up. It had been a wet season, the mud soaked into their wood and we could never get them really clean. I asked Melissa why she had buried them but she wouldn't say. I used to have morbid moods myself, as a child.

So we use the blacker dolls for villains, for wicked uncles and aunts, robbers and murderers. It's racist and will teach Melissa prejudice. She will have to come to terms with that.

When we decide what the happening is to be, we each choose dolls to play the parts. She has her favourites, I mine. There's one we both covet. It's not a doll, it's the white queen piece from a chess set. Someone has painted on a face, wings of golden hair and a simper, and two hands placidly folded, and her crown is picked out in red and green so that it looks like a hat. This figure has style, probably due to her importance on the chessboard. It sets her above the dolls. We call her Elinor.

When I'm with Melissa I'm no age. I don't look back to when I'm older. We sit on the floor in front of the little rooms and move the dolls about and speak for them. Melissa is conscious of their smallness and uses a squeaky voice. To me they are lifesize, their lives are in our hands. I don't minimise their emotions, I make them hot and cold, strong and silly. I make them bleed. If she is in a mood, Melissa makes them die.

I have to smile at the dramas we enact in Granny Appleton's little house. She wouldn't approve. Sometimes when Melissa has gone to bed I pick up the life of one or other of the dolls and go on with it, just as if it was a piece of knitting.

Melissa is not above pulling her age to get her own way. She resorts to tantrums. Once she took against Elinor. Elinor was my doll at the time, I had plans for her. Melissa started calling her 'Mrs Dumpy' and I said, 'Elinor's not married.' Melissa cried, 'She's Mrs Dumpy!' I said, 'She's not the least dumpy.' Melissa's eyes blazed, she stamped her feet, vibrating like a little engine. I said, 'Elinor's mine, I shall say what she's called.' Melissa shrieked, 'Mrs Dumpy! Mrs Dumpy!' until my throat ached for her.

The noise brought Maurice. He put his hand on Melissa's neck to quieten her. 'What's this about?'

'Melissa wants to call my doll Mrs Dumpy,' I said.

'She means Mrs Dunphy. D-U-N-P-H-Y.' I saw a schoolmaster's mouth opening round each letter as he spelled it out.

'Who?'

'Sally Dunphy's mother.'

'Who is Sally Dunphy?'

'Melissa's best friend.'

I thought I knew all Melissa's friends: Rachel and Harriet, Louise and Jennifer, Betty-Ann. I never heard of Sally Dunphy. Melissa has kept her best friend secret from me, her best has been something else from mine.

I asked her, 'Is that what you mean?' Her face went as wooden as the dolls' and she ran out of the room.

Maurice said, 'She's got a thing about Mrs Dunphy.'

'A thing?'

'She admires her.'

'What for?'

'For being a mother, I guess.'

It is possible to dislike someone you love. I found that out on my honeymoon. It was a colour print of the crucifixion which caused me to dislike Arthur, my husband.

As Mrs Winifred Appleton I had just become card-carrying. To me, in those days, a Missis, any missis, was an approved woman, fully substantiated.

The fact that I set such store by the marital status shows how green I was, sure of my importance but not of its being recognised. Arthur was supposed to take care of that. I put on him an onus which he was unaware of and unfitted for. Nobody would have been fitted for it.

I loved and was in love, and believed I had acquired a solid Establishment standing. Arthur, in becoming my husband, had achieved it for us both. On my own, plain Winnie Gibb, I'd been knocking about, waiting to be classified.

We'd gone to a ski resort for our honeymoon. Before we went, I dropped the name of the place whenever I could, brandished it into the conversation. It was something of a mouthful and to me it sounded as remote and glamorous as the Bahamas. Arthur had learned to ski, I could barely keep my balance on a kerbstone. Mr Corbishly, the consultant engineer in the firm where I worked, was the first to pick up the name. 'That's Deadsville.'

'What?'

'My daughter and son-in-law went there last January. I suppose that makes a difference.'

'What does?'

'The time of year. When the wind blows up from the valley it brings the effluvia from the factories in the plain. The smoke's so thick you never see the sun.'

'What about February?'

'My advice would be to find yourself a nice warm hotel with a good resident cook and stay indoors. The cafés are awful.' Arthur and I had booked into a pension for bed and breakfast. The idea was to eat out, sample the local restaurants and meet people. 'Alice burst into tears when she saw the place.' Mr Corbishly's telephone rang. 'Mind you, she was in an emotional state, they were on their honeymoon, and she's not strong. But you'll love it. Systems and Sanitation, Corbishly speaking.'

Arthur reassured me by asking what we had in common with Mr Corbishly's daughter and son-in-law. Marriage, I said. Arthur said it was different for us. I thought of course this is only the beginning, it's like getting born, a lot of people never manage it, but it's where you have to start.

I remembered Alice Corbishly when we got there. She was a fool, she must have been. The place was lovely, white as a swan nesting among glacial peaks that sparkled in the sun. There was no smoke, the sky was cloudless. The houses were laced with black beams, they had lattice windows and carved weather-boards painted red, green and prussian blue, like cuckoo clocks. Everywhere was puffed with snow, pure and dazzling except on the pavements where it was trodden to a caramel custard. Dinky trams buzzed to and fro, shooting sparks and ringing bells. Sledges laden with groceries, milk-cans, logs, children, cheeses, live chickens and dustbins were pushed and pulled by people and by big, high-shouldered dogs. The prevailing smell was of coffee and strawberry jam.

It was my first time abroad and I was tremendously impressed by my being there. I went round noting the different life-style, every detail of it, from the language to the lavatory-paper. Being abroad was going to change my constitution, make me cosmopolitan, it was the process of becoming legit and Arthur, my husband, was behind that. Actually he was as parochial as I was, but because he ignored the foreignness I mistook him for a man of the world.

The pension where we were to stay was wedged between a cinema and a massive rock. The rock was stuck all over with posters which had swelled with melting snow and were indecipherable. The cinema was showing 'The Hound of the Baskervilles', the pension had green shutters with heart-shaped holes and a woman in the doorway.

I'm big, but she made me look like a reed. She was about three feet across the hips. She had a breakfront bosom breaking all the way down to her knees. She stood like a monument, the only signs of life were moons of sweat on her face.

She said something I couldn't catch, it was accompanied by a crackling and creaking from her stomach or her stays, I supposed it was foreign, anyway.

Arthur said, 'Hello Mrs McSweeny.'

When we were in our room with the door shut I said, 'Why didn't you tell me?'

'Tell you what?'

'She's English!'

'She would be. They come from East Grinstead.'

'I had a right to know.'

'A right?'

'We're husband and wife, we're not supposed to keep things from each other.'

'What things?'

'Don't keep repeating me!' It struck me that we were on the brink of our first married quarrel.

'This is no thing, this is old Mrs McSweeny who takes in boarders and it doesn't matter a damn whether she's a Serbo-Croat or Scotch-Irish.' He started kissing my neck.

Of course we had had differences before, our minds

didn't always dovetail, even when our bodies did. '*Post coitum tristus est*' applied to me, whereas Arthur became practical and forward-looking. Before we were married he used to map out our lives, and when we got a home of our own he concentrated on immediate matters like re-siting the garden shed or panelling the loft.

I had expected a radical change to take effect with the marriage service. I was *devout* the day I got married. I believed that every word the vicar said was sacred: 'Do you, Arthur Frederick Appleton, take this woman to be your lawful wedded wife, forsaking all others?' All others weren't just women, they were anything and everything I couldn't go along with.

Arthur was having trouble with the zipper of my going-away dress. 'What matters,' I said, 'is you not knowing what matters.'

'You have to trust me. For as long as we both shall live.'

I saw that there was more than one way of making a change, and had my first intimation of the chicanery of marriage. But I also saw the potential, which was a nicely adjusted give and take, years of happy dealing. I helped with the zip. We were on the bed, I on my back, interested in what Arthur was doing, when I looked up at the picture.

A man can be pitiable and still be a man, like this one, his thighs stretched to breaking point and his feet fastened by a twelve-inch nail through his insteps and another through each wrist. This man had had the final affront to bear: indifference. It had finished him. A hand can curl up and die.

I pummelled Arthur's chest. He thought I was impatient and turned pale with anxiety. I cried no, no, stop—don't—twisting my head to and fro, hitting him on the chin with my chin and nearly knocking us both out. When he understood I wasn't inciting, but demurring, he pushed himself up on his arms and stared at me.

'I can't,' I said, 'not in front of that.' He looked over

his shoulder, and saw the picture. I moaned. 'I'll never be able to here.'

Arthur has a natural dignity at unnatural moments. He rose up from the bed, lifted the picture off the wall, put it in the cupboard and came back and we forgot everything. That's how it should be, you should have revelations, not memories.

Next morning he had me up early and out. I stood in the snow while he sorted his equipment. 'First thing to remember,' he said, 'is there's a right and a wrong way to carry your skis. You put them on your shoulder with the tips pointing forward, with more ski in front than behind you. They're balanced that way.'

I'd always thought honeymooners spent the first day of their honeymoon in bed, but hadn't liked to say so. It seemed, well, lascivious.

'Look,' he said. I was looking at the snow. When I say snow I don't mean those little white poultices we get at home. This stuff was king: houses, people, trees, everything else had to poke through. You wouldn't know that place without the snow, any more than you'd know a man you'd only ever seen with shaving cream all over his face. But this wasn't like shaving cream, this had consistency, billions of consistent tons packed up to the sky.

'What's that?' I said, pointing.

'An alp,' said Arthur. 'Never swing round suddenly when you're carrying your skis, you could give someone a nasty box on the ears. What you do, in lift queues or just standing, is drop your skis to the ground tail first—'

'I haven't got any skis.'

'We'll hire some for you. But not today. Not your first day.'

'So what shall we do? Take a sleigh ride?'

'Look.' He was looking at the alp, I couldn't tell what he was thinking, my bridegroom. 'This is your first day—' he didn't say *our* first day, though it was our first ever, and not to be repeated—'you must get acclimatised, get the feel of it.'

'It's not easy to keep your feel when you're half frozen.'

'You're tired, that's what it is.' He put his arm round me, nibbled my ear. 'Isn't it?'

'Why should it be? This is our first day, but last night wasn't our first night.'

'That's what I mean, the wedding, the fuss, the journey. It builds up. I want you fresh tomorrow, because tomorrow I'll take you on the beginners' slopes.'

'What shall we do today?' I said again, but not dogged, it was too early for the early warning system.

'Rest. Find a nice warm place and wait for me.'

'Wait?'

'With a hot chocolate and apple-strudel. How does that strike you?'

'I've just had breakfast.'

'I shan't be long, an hour or so.'

'Where are you going?'

'To the top of the Grosspitz.'

'What spits?'

He pointed to the alp which was like an ice-cream cone with ice-cream all over. 'I want to try the run down from the glacier. See if I still can.'

I saw the headlines: 'Bride of a day widowed on honeymoon'. 'Suppose you can't?'

'Winnie, it's wonderful, there's no sensation like it, it's out of this world—you go like a bullet, no wings. Before we leave here we'll be skiing down the piste together. I promise you.'

To cut the story shorter, he went, carrying his skis the right way, balanced on his shoulder, and I trailed after him as far as the ski-lift.

'Wait for me!' he called unnecessarily as the thing moved off and up. It was full of whooping and horsing men. I watched until it was no bigger than a bobbin on a thread.

'Makes you puke,' said a girl standing next to me.

'Oh my husband's a good skier.' I put a lot into that, a whole happy married life. 'I don't grudge him his fun.'

'What turns me over is they don't check the cable runs,' said the girl, gloomily shifting something in her jaw. 'The brakes burn out and the whole can of beans comes down—*zat*! Six thousand feet's quite a spread, you know, and they don't reckon to find everything till the snow's gone.'

'You shouldn't come here if that's how you feel.'

'How I feel is if I face it, it won't happen.'

'I know that feeling. Who have you got up there?'

'No one.'

'In the lift I mean.'

It wasn't gum she was chewing, it was a nervous fidget. 'I'm waiting for the butterflies to settle.' It crossed my mind that I was fated, among other things, to pick up with nutters. I didn't feel like encouraging her. Then she said, 'They're in my stomach. I love to ski but I'm scared of heights. It's always like this on the first day.'

'It's my first day too.'

'I'll be OK tomorrow. I have to be, I can't afford to waste time.'

'Are you good at skiing?'

'Reasonably.'

'Would you teach me?'

'You've got to be joking.'

'You could give me a few hints, like what and what not to do. While you're waiting for the butterflies.' I saw it all, I do see these things: Arthur coming back and me astonishing him with my grasp of the sport, or whatever it's called. 'You're a natural!' he'd cry, and then we could go to bed.

'Sorry.' She walked away, she had reflectors on her boots, and I was left with my original scenario of the deserted bride.

Arthur came down off the mountain, his little gold moustache shining in his rosy face. 'Did you see me?' He looked bridal and I knew I didn't. 'On the slalom?'

I lied because he was so happy and the mother in me couldn't disappoint the child who had just proved he could ride his bike on one wheel. 'Yes, I saw you wave.'

'Wave? On the *slalom*?'

'It was you, I knew your red cap.'

'Everyone's got a red cap.'

It was true—everyone except the ones who liked to have their hair freeze. He didn't really care whether I'd seen him or not, because all that mattered was that he had done it. And there was me, not even aware of what it was, exactly, that he had done.

He stood laughing and vibrant, arms outstretched, hands resting on his ski-sticks and I thought of that picture over our bed. There was no revelation, I was simply and bluntly acquainted with the fact of the likeness and the difference between Arthur and the man on the cross.

Don't misunderstand: Arthur was good enough, and more, for me. I never wanted him to be a saint or a martyr. Or God. But something got to me, a disgrace that was wholly mine. Arthur's, if he had any, was another matter, and none of my business. This was made crystal and coldly clear, along with the other surprises, not only to say shocks, I had coming to me. 'Oh God, the picture!'

'Picture?'

'The one we took off the wall and never put back. It's still in the cupboard.'

'So?'

'What will they think?'

'That we're not religious,' he said cheerfully.

'They might not have missed it yet—if we go back now we could hang it up—'

'After lunch we'll go back.' He came close, made a triangle with his skis and penned me in. 'There'll be no point, then, in hanging it up.'

We found the picture gone from the cupboard. In its place on the wall was another, of a voluptuous baby with a three-ring halo and the smile of the Mona Lisa.

II

MRS MCSWEENY, CALLED as she is to rise in the dark and shatter it with lights in order to cut bread and fill milk jugs (early morning tea she draws the line at, from incapacity not unwillingness, she simply could not climb and re-climb the stairs half a dozen times more every morning, a dozen it would be, counting the collection of the trays), Mrs McSweeny has still to acquire her purpose in life. She was relieved of one which she had when her periods stopped. Her husband still hopes, he believes that God moves in mysterious ways. Menstruation is mystery enough for her.

She has always been well-dispersed, outlying rather than remote, and it takes time for her to get herself together. Concentration being gradual, she does not readily tackle problems or answer questions. She finds they sort themselves without her.

After the end of her expectations, she soldiered on with the common round and daily task. That is quite enough: her purpose (the one she was relieved of) was altogether too much. When at last—it could be any time between ten p.m. and midnight—she is able to take the weight off her knees, she sits with those knees wide apart, reflecting how unequal she was to it.

Murdo, her husband, is a different temperament: inspired. She has to live with his inspiration. It is a trying time, she has tried, and been tried. The time factor supported her, for surely, she thought, somehow it would come right. Then time expired in her forty-fifth year. Without symptoms or premonitions the business ceased. In another woman it could have been ground for hope, another woman would have been entitled to hope and could have excused herself by attributing a false pregnancy to the whim and wisdom of God, a last-minute reversal. Mrs McSweeny—Eileen as she had been named, never Mary—has no such resource.

Murdo has kept going, though he no longer hears voices, only rustlings which he interprets as 'soon' and 'search'. Mrs McSweeny has asked does he know what he should search for. 'Search and ye shall find—' he left it at that.

A girl here on her honeymoon says, 'We're sorry about the picture. It didn't seem right. To leave it on the wall, I mean.'

She aims the words, paling rather than blushing, and Mrs McSweeny receives them between the eyes and is reminded that she has no purpose. Since losing Murdo's, she has continued to grow like a tree, big and bigger, displacing more and more air, taking up more and more room. She has nothing in mind, no function other than to keep going which, for her, means keeping others going.

'I'll fetch you more bread.' She has seen the girl's husband take the last piece.

'It's got spunk,' he says appreciatively. 'Not like steamed flannel.'

'It's the seeds in it.'

The girl, for some reason, colours up.

Not one to associate ideas, Mrs McS starts to receive some unsolicited memories. They come between her and the ham she is frying. She is unable to cope with the past and the present together. She drops an egg, stares blankly at a coffeepot smoking dry on the stove, and forgets the honeymooners' bread. The man signals with the empty basket. It looks to her like a cradle. Tomorrow she will have help.

But she cannot be sure. Murdo says he has found someone. She will be the same girl who has so often come into Mrs McSweeny's kitchen carrying her burden, her hair in the curly drizzle of young people everywhere. Mrs McS will call her 'love' out of pity, and because she has to live with Murdo's inspiration. And because she never knows.

It is getting more and more difficult to find pregnant girls willing to work. There are so many opportunities for them nowadays. If they are prepared to sweep the crumbs off the tables, they expect to be pampered. None of them stays to the end of her term. They become bored or nervous, or someone fetches them away. They feel overpowered by Mrs McSweeny. She is monolithic and appears to lack human emotion. And Murdo spooks them. He is full of crazy ideas. They decide that he is nuts. A natural assumption. They giggle and become manipulators, twist him round their fingers along with their screw-curls.

Murdo's ideas are about the final scenario, the moment the world is dying for. He fears the world may die with all its sins upon it before the moment comes. How should he prepare? There are considerations which he, as a hotelier, must consider.

He started by putting up a shed in the yard. He thatched it himself, though not well—thatching not being his trade—and put in a couple of stalls for beasts, but no beasts. The inn he has, this is to be the stable.

He knows about the immaculate conception and he has read about an immaculate delivery: queens and princesses sitting on gilded thrones and discussing politics while they give birth. Just in case, he has removed the bed from the best bedroom and put in its place a high-backed chair of carved mahogany and Spanish leather. The only other thing in the room is a hostess trolley draped with a length of beautiful old and smelly brocaded velvet. He thinks it might be useful, and certainly it is appropriate. But no girl has stayed to take advantage of the preparations.

Mrs McSweeny is remembering East Grinstead. It is a lifetime away, a dream which she cherishes, recreating for her troubled flesh the mild winters and wet summers of that verdant place. She thinks of it as other people think of holidays, unending pleasure in Paradise sustained. There were no drawbacks in East Grinstead. She sees herself, a young woman, standard-size, at the door of her semi, waving goodbye to her husband as he leaves for work, herself one of the wives shopping at Sainsbury's, making the double bed—only the one—or returning to it until nine and longer if she wishes. She remembers the strong English green, cool but not bitter, moist but not slushy. East Grinstead is her idea of heaven. She knows that it is inferior to Murdo's, but hopes that as there will be many mansions in the Father's house there will be many heavens and she will be allowed hers.

Not being fanciful or informed about such matters she had supposed, when first he spoke of hearing voices, that they were the neighbours'. But when she put her ear to the party-wall and said she could hear next door's Hoover, he became violently angry, something she had never known him be before. From that moment he was a changed man. And Mrs McSweeny, not wishing, not prepared for, scarcely aware of the possibility of change, was lost.

She operates in a tight circle, gingerly doing those things which she must, leaving aside all else, the might-have-beens, the yens, the fancies she is entitled to. She is unthinking but not thoughtless. Biding her time, or Murdo's, she goes about her small business, an elephant balancing on a pail.

Murdo, listening more and more to his voices, listened less and less to his wife. If she spoke, he shushed her. The voices were faint, he said, and could not take competition with her chatter. Mrs McS, who never chattered, was shamed.

It was a long time before he would tell her what the voices were saying to him. It was Bible-talk, he said, which she wouldn't understand.

The voices came at any time, while he was at his dinner or with shaving lather in his earholes or doing his pools, though not when he was listening to the sports round-up. They also came at those times when married people rely on being unchallenged. Murdo would raise his head from

Mrs McSweeny's breast crying 'Listen!' and she would try to still the beating of her heart.

They weren't churchgoers. She had stopped saying her prayers because Murdo did not like to be kept waiting after he was in bed. And he called on God under provocation, without expecting direct intervention or feeling resentment when it did not come.

Mrs McSweeny, seeing his rapt expression, his eager nods, his hand uplifted to enjoin silence as he listened to the voices, scented danger. She could not envisage what form it would take, and when he finally told her what the voices were saying, she felt crushing fear.

'It will be on the twenty-first of August, in a place of licence and self-seeking. Some place with a foreign name.'

'Like Tesco's?' She had meant to be helpful, but it was made clear at the outset that in this matter she would be helpless.

Murdo gave her a look of acid rage. 'I must be there.'

She dared to say, 'But where?'

'I'll be told.'

It was then the fifteenth of July. Her birthday was on the thirtieth. He took her to a Happy Eater and they had steak and crinkle chips and passion-fruit sundaes. Over the ice-cream he told her that the place was in the Alps. He enunciated the name carefully, it sounded like swearing and she was no wiser. 'It's in Germany,' he said, 'where we're going.'

'We?'

'You want to be there when it happens, don't you?'

It was the last thing she wanted: if it was going to happen she wanted to be as far away as possible. She was frightened, for herself and for the world. Like at the coming of a nuclear holocaust. She could not say so to Murdo.

Murdo was changed from the steady, placable man who had enjoyed life and extended his simple pleasures to anyone who could share them. He was on fire, he gawked at her out of an inner blaze. Like the bush in the Bible, he burned and was not consumed. She did think sometimes that he might be asking for help: he turned up the whites of his eyes, begging, she thought, to be saved from the flames. 'Come and lie down,' she said, 'lie down with me and we'll draw the curtains.' Her idea was that he would be better in the dark. But he raised his fists, silent and dreadful, as if to curse her, and she did not try again. First and last, she was afraid of him.

They went on August 18 so as to be in good time, and she was unable to pronounce the name of the place even when she saw it written up. It has to be spat out and she couldn't get her lips to do it.

She neither liked nor disliked the place, she was affrighted, as anyone would be. If it *was* the appointed place, chosen—like the other—without rhyme or reason or evident qualification, then every brick, tile, flake of its wood and grain of its dirt was momentous. The moment was coming that would make it so.

Nothing happened. The voices kept telling them to wait. Very tedious she found it. Murdo paced up and down their hotel room and haunted the streets. People objected to him peering into their windows, standing tranced on their doorsteps, listening to their conversations.

He had Mrs McSweeny watching with him from midnight on the twentieth. They watched for the star which he said would come from behind the mountain, slowly, slowly descend into the town, to hang directly over the birthplace. They watched until dawn, until the sky was bright with sun. Murdo said a ball of fire would roll down the mountainside, demolishing the ski lifts, burning all in its path.

He stood cracking his knuckles and his jawbone, a habit he had lately formed. He went into the street and held up his arms. People buffeted him as they passed. Mrs McS packed their bags.

In the afternoon a billy-goat broke loose and held a woman at bay in a telephone kiosk. There were no more disturbances until the beer and burger bars closed and the young were cast upon the streets. The noise they made was the same as Sodom and Gomorrah's. Worn out, Murdo put his face in Mrs McSweeny's lap and wept.

Although the voices stopped talking to him, he insisted they wait for the rest of the week, during which time there was total silence. Mrs McSweeny hoped that what it was, had been, it was now over. And done with. She watched Murdo, bested and bruised, relapse into himself. They returned home and her thankfulness was so great she could have cried.

But the voices had got back to East Grinstead first. They spoke as soon as Murdo got inside the front door. Just the one word, the name of the village in the mountains which Mrs McS couldn't pronounce.

'It's got to be there!' cried Murdo. Mrs McSweeny felt like panicking. Their lives were threatened and so perhaps were everyone else's, but if nothing happened, everyone else would have a chance. She and Murdo were doomed either way. 'We've got to stay there until it happens.'

'We just left.'

'We must go back.'

'I'm going to make some tea.' The pot of tea was all she had to put between her and that place.

Murdo sold their house and furniture and the car, everything except their clothes. In despair she asked, 'Shan't we ever come home again?' He said they didn't need a home. 'But where are we going to live?' He said in the light of the world.

Greatly daring, she disassociated herself from Murdo's voices and tried listening for some of her own. She was probably as in need of redemption as the next person (though she had never been one for mischief). What she couldn't understand was why they had to go to that place for it. She had looked in vain for signs of lust and licence, which by Murdo's reckoning should be rampant. There was haggling in the marketplace, women gossipping, drunks, and a lecherous goat, but what was so special about it?

She did get an answer to that, not a spoken one, it organised itself and came to her. Bethlehem, in the beginning, had been nothing to write home about. Had she been a thinking woman she might have reflected that the quality of sin had advanced since then and there might be some enormity too compounded to be apparent to the earthly eye. As it was, the answer simply led her to ask why not East Grinstead, and on that one she remained unenlightened.

'We must find lodgings and get work,' said Murdo.

'Work?'

'For both of us. We can't afford to live in hotels. It's not a holiday.'

In desolation, sick of heart and stomach, she rode for the last time on a green bus to Gatwick.

She had been christened Eileen, never Mary. The voices did not tell him that she was to give the birth. That knowledge grew inside him he said. She did not miss the way he phrased it, she had a monstrous vision of scheduled growths, of which the voices were the first. Others would follow, overtaking each other, crowding out the man and his good nature, the easy-going, common-sensical man she had loved and married.

'My dear,' she said, he was still hers to fear, 'My dear, do you know what you're saying?'

What matters is what he believes, and he still believes she could give birth, though she is forty-nine years old and weighs twenty stone. She thinks her fatness is a punishment for letting him down. Sometimes she tries to imagine what might have happened if she had had a child. Any child. What their lives would have been, Murdo waiting and watching for holiness, super-powers, allowing no margin for error or nappy-rash. She shudders.

But Murdo amasses hope. He is radiant with it. If not her, it will be someone else. He follows every pregnant woman with his eyes, and on his feet. He is suspected of perversion, he has been warned and threatened by husbands, sweethearts, parents and blood relatives. The more spirited mothers-to-be have themselves rounded on him. He is unpopular, so is Mrs McS because she is his wife.

None of this concerns the people come for the skiing, and the McSweenys make enough taking in winter visitors to keep them solvent through the summer. Murdo has little interest in the business, he is out a lot, carrying his belief like a torch, burning but unconsumed. So long as he is not dogging the footsteps of a pregnant girl, he is good for a laugh as the local weirdo. In the season others, weirder and wonderful, flock into the town to entertain the holiday-makers. Murdo, then, is ignored. Even when he goes to order supplies, cash in hand, he is made to wait.

The running of the pension is left to Mrs McSweeny. She needs help, but girls do not stay. Murdo frightens them with his burning stare and reaching hands—a man who never touches his wife.

Perhaps Joseph touched Mary, it would require only a minor miracle to cancel or sanctify the act. But Murdo has not been advised, and he knows there would be nothing immaculate about his touch. So he leaves his wife alone, and they both suffer.

Mrs McSweeny assures the honeymooner, the man signalling with the bread basket which looks like a cradle, 'Tomorrow there'll be someone.'

*

I suppose it's conceivable, the way we're going, that one day we'll be able to handle genesis, climate and galactic government. But what about degrees of wickedness, how shall we assess them? I don't mean the stabs we make now, probation for the woman who steals a pair of tights and a fine for the man who drinks and drives. I'm thinking of the wages of sin et al, paradise, purgatory, perdition, breast-beating, who goes where.

I'm thinking of my mother-in-law. Where does she fit in? The way her original sin has developed has made her the wickedest woman I know. She's no better and no worse than mass-murderers, and the girl who went round tempting people to torture and burn her so that she could be a martyr. We shall have to take care of all that when we have cracked genesis.

Mrs Appleton Senior's grain of mischief has grown into an organised crime. As her son's wife, I'm a prime target. She has fun with the others, me she's serious about.

'Poor old Dad,' Arthur said once—it was when I was starting to have what I still thought of as dishonourable doubts about her—'married to a good woman.' We were in bed at the time, enjoying ourselves.

'What am I?' I said.

He laughed. 'Human.'

He thinks she's too good to be true. She can't be true because he thinks of her as men think of women, leaving out what they can't be reconciled or bothered with. Even I wouldn't condemn her to such a half-fleshed existence. But it would embarrass Arthur to fill her in: he has canonised her to suit himself.

She makes waves on the bosom of the family. (Mind you, our bosom was never peaceful.) Even cousins in Australia, even prospective members feel the wash.

Her method is perfect for the material. We are Mrs Appleton Senior's material. It has taken acumen to restrict herself to us. In the family she has all she needs for her operations. You'd think there's enough trouble without her making more. But we all make trouble for someone, just by living.

Appletons come of a solid West Country stock, it would take more than her machinations to break them up and anyway, that's not what she wants. She wants to be a backroom matriarch. Her machinations are intended to make waves to wash someone away. Me, for instance.

'When we were kids,' said Arthur, 'we all sat down

every Sunday at one o'clock to roast and three veg, batter pudding, stewed fruit and custard. She can't forget.'

He thinks she lives in the past, pinafore-time, and can see him as the rough-headed boy he still is at heart. That's a deep, delicate area which only she can cater for.

Let me tell you about last Sunday. It was all arranged, she arranged it with what she had in mind, which was some sort of demonstration about me, my housekeeping, my bad-wifery. All she needed to do was assemble the audience and something was bound to come up. The audience was to be Arthur's young brother who was bringing his girl Delphine, and Arthur's uncle Jack who was bringing Arthur's aunt, Arthur's father, Maurice, Melissa, and Arthur, with herself and me in the leading parts.

I had the meal ready to serve at one o'clock: sirloin with Yorkshire pudding and horseradish cream, roast potatoes, brussels and string beans, Dutch apple-tart and chocolate mould to follow. The table was set for ten and I made the napkins into cocked hats. Arthur warned me that Uncle Jack would put his on his head, being the family joker.

She arrived at twelve-thirty. Arthur's father is bigger than she is, but I only get glimpses of him when he's with her.

She starts as soon as she gets inside the door. 'Winnie, that's another pretty dress, it's even prettier than the one you wore at Christmas.'

'It is the one I wore at Christmas.'

'I wish I had your knack of finding the right clothes. Everything looks lovely on you, but then you're tall.'

After that we sit drinking sherry: 'Only a toothful for me,' she says, 'I know my limitations.'

She tells Arthur he is putting on weight and it suits him. I've seen him stripped and I know it doesn't. At ten minutes to one she remarks how good the roast smells and I say I hope the others won't be much longer. 'Others?' she sounds bemused, though she has had a very small sherry. I go to the window and twitch the curtains.

'Uncle Jack and Aunt Betty,' Arthur obliges.

'But they aren't coming.' I stand with my hand on the curtain, holding on. 'Didn't you know?'

Arthur says we didn't.

'The last thing Betty said was shall I tell Winnie or shall you.'

'Nobody told me,' I say.

'Are you sure?'

'Why aren't they coming?'

'I don't really know. Betty said they couldn't, and she'd tell me why later. She was so worried about what you'd think. I said it couldn't be helped and you'd understand it was one of those things.'

'What things?'

'With the best will in the world things go wrong.' Faced with the possibility that I am not ready to understand, she decides I can do with a little philosophy. 'I always think every plan we make is a hostage to fortune.' This is Mills and Boon country and I say nothing. 'And the children have gone to Alton Towers.'

'What children?'

'Ernest and Delphine.'

'What towers?'

'The leisure park. They had the chance of going with friends and it was too good to miss. It's so much fun for young people. They asked if I thought you'd mind.'

'They didn't ask me.'

'Of course I knew you wouldn't.' She smiles at all of us, me especially because me she knows and everyone has to believe what she leads them to believe she knows about me. 'I told them, go while you've got the chance. I think young ones should get out and about with people their own age, don't you?'

'I mind, I definitely mind being stood up for a fun fair.' She glows under her dusty pink Phul-Nana. (She showers it over her face and neck with a swansdown puff on a stick. No one seeing her do that would think she has a grain of guile in her.) 'I'll tell you what I think,' I say, 'I think it's bloody discourteous.' Arthur grins, so does his father, sheepish. 'Not one word of apology or regret from any of them.'

'Oh my dear—'

'What worries me is how creepy my own kids are going to sound because I have brought them up to say please and thank you.'

'You mustn't believe that. They said they were sorry, they all said so!'

'Not to me. If two of them, Ernest or Delphine, and Betty or Jack, had rung up and said "We're sorry", I might have asked what about and it might just have come out that they weren't coming to lunch and I shouldn't have prepared for ten when we're only going to be six.'

'Leave it, Win,' says Arthur.

'On second thoughts I'd rather not hear it from Jack because he laughs when he says he's sorry. Of course it's academic now, but I should like to believe someone was sorry.'

Arthur's father says 'Olga told you they weren't coming.' (Olga is Mrs Appleton Senior.)

'I said to Norman I must ring Winnie and let her know. Didn't I, Norman?'

'That's what you said.'

Arthur says, 'Those of us who are here are ready to eat. So let's eat.'

'Nobody rang me.'

She looks from one to the other of them, at everyone except me. 'I could have sworn I did.' She registers disbelief, disquiet, dismay, in the right pecking order. 'I was so sure—but if you say I didn't I suppose—I must have—forgotten—' She knows when to go to pieces. 'Oh dear, my silly head, my memory lets me down. I'm getting old!'

Arthur glowers at me. 'She probably did tell you, and what with one thing and another it slipped your mind.'

'What thing and another?'

'For God's sake let's *all* forget it. Go and dish up.'

He thinks I'm making a fuss about nothing because old

people forget all the time. They're phasing out, forgetting is no crime.

I caught sight of him in the Park, when I had thought he was at his club where he goes to play billiards and talk about Mrs Thatcher.

He was with a girl, nobody I know, but I don't know any girls, only women my own age. I hear you ask: what age is that? You've been reading the newspapers: 'Woman, 54, crashes Ford Sierra, eighteen months, into listed oak, six hundred and fifty years old.'

I was some distance away, and naturally I took care they shouldn't see me, it comes naturally to spy on your husband. As far as I could make out, the girl was neither a dolly nor a frightnik. She had long hair and a tweed jacket which didn't harmonise with her flowered skirt. Maurice would call her trad.

Arthur was dancey at her side—he is, or used to be, when he's excited, but he hasn't been dancey with me for years.

While we were having breakfast next morning I told him I'd seen him in the Park. I don't believe in beating about the bush and I'd lost sleep wondering about the girl.

Arthur was spared from reacting by the toaster popping up. I said, 'Who was she?'

'Who was who?'

'Who you were with.'

'Oh, just someone I met on my train.'

She wouldn't have liked the tone he said it in, throwaway, for my benefit. He calls the eight-fifteen to the City his because he travels on it five days a week.

'So you met her again in the Park.'

'On my way to the club.'

'The club's in the other direction.'

'I was taking a walk, I like to walk in the Park, it's the only green space we have.'

'I don't think of you as a country boy.'

'After sitting at a desk all day I like to stretch my legs. Anything wrong with that?'

'It's lovely.'

He said, 'If you're thinking, don't. Save yourself the trouble. I happened to be in the Park, she happened to be in the Park, we recognised each other and walked as far as the rose garden together. Then she went her way, wherever that was, and I went to the club.'

'The rose garden.' I sighed, I really put into that sigh. I mean, you don't need to know your husband if you know men and you know about the rose garden. It's a reasonable place to walk to and this one occupies a third of the area, you can't very well miss it if you're walking in the Park. I asked myself, if he had said they walked as far as the bottle-bank and no farther would I have believed him. The answer was yes. My sigh was full of meaning.

Arthur didn't see it. He delivered a swift peck to my cheek and said he was going or he'd be late. Referring to the clock I would have said he had ample time and I was left with a further consideration, was he rushing away because he had something to hide.

While it's true you don't need to know your husband, and the broad general picture of mankind which confronts you daily will suffice, a few relevancies are useful. In twenty years of marriage I have learned that Arthur avoids confrontation, that he would rather be too early than late and he isn't a breakfast eater. On balance I had to allow him, and myself, the benefit of the doubt.

III

ARTHUR HAS GIVEN UP hope of adventures on the train but he remains open to opportunity. He sits with his knees evenly spread, he is tidy, unlike me—I reckon to pick up on my way back. He goes through his paper, getting the burden of the main news items. I know for a fact that when he gets to his office they spend the first half hour over coffee and the leaders.

He turns to the crossword. Then the girl next to him asks how many stops to London Bridge.

'Eight,' he says, 'seven after this one.'

She says she hadn't thought it was so many. He says there are more stops on the loop. What loop, she says, and he explains about the Junction. He must think she's stupid she says, the fact is they've only just moved to this district and this is her first time on the eight-fifteen. She glances at his newspaper and says six down must be 'make-believe'. Arthur doesn't like being told the answers to his crossword. However, she seems intelligent and to want to talk.

She's a quarter of a century younger than he is, she's had twenty-five years less to think and that makes her enviable.

Arthur begins to notice how smooth her hands are, no bones, dimples instead of knuckles. He asks where she's moved to and it turns out it's the next road from ours. He tells her what a nice area she's come to: pleasant, well-planned, good-class houses—it's permissible to say that of houses, but being careful he adds 'well-built'—good shopping centre, transport facilities and, he smiles with real warmth, 'nice people'.

Is there any country, she says, so he tells her about our Park, what a lovely park it is, spacious and well-kept, though there's a reservation for grass and flowers and trees to grow at will and it's possible to believe you're in wildest Surrey.

Where is this park, she says, and Arthur explains how to get there and what to look for when she does. She mustn't miss the Seasonal Clock, laid out differently for each quarter of the year. In spring it's stuffed with hyacinths, daffodils, snowdrops, gentians, and the hands stand at fifteen minutes past the hour. Summer it's a blaze of geraniums, lupins, Indian Shot, vulgaria and Schizophilla, and the hands point to half past the year. In autumn the year's three-quarters gone and we get asters, chrysanths and dahlias. In winter there are hardy heathers and creepers to keep it going, and by Christmas the hands reach the top of the dial and are reinforced with holly, mistletoe and silver balls.

Then there's the maze, a tricky bit of arboriculture. People go in there to be alone, if you know what I mean. When they find there isn't room for two breast to breast they're resentful and kick the bushes down. Then there's the bowling green, he tells her about that though she's not of an age to play bowls. Then there's the lake. He tells her it's a lake though it's more of a pond. She says she hopes it's cleaner than the lake she saw in Switzerland. Arthur says of course it's on a small scale, but she should see the water irises in bloom.

The girl decides to impart what is almost a confidence. Arthur has reminded her of something she has put aside, but she is ready to look at it again in his company. Talking about it to an unknown man met on the train, personless as far as she is concerned, will put it into perspective. Make it assimilable. It is, after all, a past experience and its significance is self-evident, goes without saying. She doesn't need to be saying it, but she thinks if she does the memory will fall into its proper place. Which is tucked down somewhere in her subconscious.

'My grandmother used to tell me about this place. She went when she was a girl, with her governess—can you believe it! French conversation, silk gloves, brown button boots. She smelled lovely, my grandmother, sort of creamy.' The girl tries to look out of the window which is steamed over. She mustn't lose sight, not now. She holds the picture fixed this side of the dirty glass, superimposed on a notice about Aids counselling. 'When she went there the lake was clean and nice. A man cycled round it three times a day, keeping the weed down. He had a wooden rake and he raked the weeds and any rubbish to the shore and another man came in a donkey-cart and took it away. People didn't throw things in the water, they carried their chocolate papers to the litter baskets. There weren't any beer or Coke tins. Beautiful white swans lived on an island, they came gliding across the water like royalty approaching. The water was so clear my grandmother said you could see down to the bottom and when a worm moved it sent up a little plume like smoke. The way she described it made a big impression on me. I kept it in mind—you know what I mean?—it was something nice to think about. Well, this summer, I decided to really go and see it. It would be just like she said, I thought, and I practically thought I'd see her walking about wearing her gloves and button boots. You've got to believe it.' The girl utters a small snort. 'Well, the lake was full of rubbish, tins, bottles, cartons, newspapers, tyres—terrible things. There was oil too, nobody keeping it clean. The poor swans were all grey and jaded, they broke the scum and when it closed up behind them flies hopped about on it.'

Arthur tuts sympathetically. He wants her to know we're not like that. Our Park is what such places are supposed to be, a public garden for everyone's pleasure and relaxation. We take care of it, we don't allow it to be abused—not consistently. There will always be some thoughtless or bloody-minded element out to spoil what others enjoy—

'The Swiss blame the tourists. They called us pigs.'
'Really?'

'Really!' she snaps, rather unfairly relating some of her bad feeling to Arthur, 'and I don't like being called "Miss Piggy".'

'Actually, it's the other side of the picture.'

'What picture?'

'It's the bloody-minded element, perverts and morons out to screw things up. In their case their own economy.'

'I didn't spoil their lake, they did.'

'That's what I mean. They're cutting off their noses to spite their faces. Tourism is their main source of revenue.'

She turns to rub the steam off the window, looks for a new perspective. Her grandmother's lake is still there, still high priority. So is Miss Piggy, simpering porker in high-heeled shoes and a plunge neckline.

Arthur thinks they have strayed from his subject. It becomes a matter of importance to keep the girl's attention, a minor social, intellectual, and sexual challenge, all the more challenging in the context of this crowded compartment of the eight-fifteen.

'Think you'll like living in Cremona Crescent?' She shrugs. 'It's a nice road. Did you know it's named after the River Crem? Which has been driven underground. It comes up in the Park, you can see the current flowing in at the eastern end of the lake, a solid belt of water. That old river would drag you down with it to the sea if it wasn't well and truly buried.'

She gives him a flickering look. 'I thought the road was named after the Italian town.'

'It's not generally known that we live on what was once an extensive wetland. Several streams converge into the Crem and the Crem meets the Thames at Putney.'

That's news to me. Arthur goes on to explain why we don't find any mention in the official guide, he says because the planners and developers don't want to advertise the fact that our town is built on a marsh.

The train stops at the Junction and the carriage fills. It's standing-room only, shoulder to shoulder, elbow to ribs, the standing-up feet on the sitting-down feet. A man standing on Arthur's feet talks over Arthur's head.

'It was fantastic. Out of this world.'

'Into it you mean,' says the man next to him.

'A fantastic experience. Not one I'd recommend before breakfast.'

'Gruesome?'

'Hell no, I mean it was Sally, wasn't it? And she was glad to have me there. She said I helped.'

'Cutting cords and what not?'

'Can you see me?' They both laugh.

Arthur speaks in a private voice. 'Not that you need worry about flooding, it's all taken care of. You may notice we have more manholes and catchment grilles than other places. There's a pumping station behind the bus depot.'

The girl looks up at the man on Arthur's feet. Arthur goes on to point out that it's therapeutic living over water, the currents exert magnetic influences. That's the first I've heard of it. Are there currents in marshes? He can still surprise me.

The girl is eavesdropping on the overhead conversation. The second man says: 'They asked me to be present when Fiona came along. Parental involvement they call it. I couldn't face it, I said I'd got an AGM to go to.'

'You missed a bloody miracle—to coin a phrase.'

'I had actually got an AGM. Anyway, Chloe didn't want me there.'

Arthur is soldiering on. 'When you see a water-diviner at work you realise the power of water. Not only the brute force, it has a physical and mental influence. After all, if you think about it, water was our first element. It still covers seven-tenths of the earth's surface and geologically speaking we've only just crawled out.'

'The face was up instead of down,' says the man over Arthur's head. 'A complication, apparently. I didn't enjoy that.' He catches the girl's eye. 'The end product didn't seem to justify the hanky-panky poor old Sal went through. Blue-raw and slimy it was, like a bad oyster.'

He smiles down at the girl and she smiles up at him.

*

When we were first married Arthur hated leaving me to go to work. He used to write notes and leave them about the house where I'd find them after he'd gone. He wrote things like: 'I'm remembering last night.' 'Did I tell you I love you?' 'I want to be with you all the time.'

He's still capable of it, he hasn't changed. But I have. I'm not what he wants, I'm not what he married.

I look in the mirror: there I am, mapped out, a featured plain due north; having to wash and tidy and occasionally try to tart it up, I know it better than the back of my hand. Then come two hills which engross wool, cotton and man-made fibres; my dresses are recognisable on the hanger by their bust displacement. Then comes a broad central area, somewhat tumescent, giving on to a deep, deep valley. My legs were never my best feature, I don't look at them. My arms disgust me, the flesh from shoulder to elbow quakes. I have dowager's arms. It doesn't make Arthur unfaithful, it makes me expendable.

But not my soul. Some people came to save it, they knocked on the door, rat-a-tat-tat, crisp and efficient. They could have been a recorded delivery. I found two men and a woman huddled in my porch to escape the rain.

'Honey,' said the woman, a Jamaican, 'is your life burdensome?'

'No place to turn?' inquired one of the men, who was white.

'Not knowing the Word of God.'

'The Great Logos.'

'His mercy.'

'His vengeance.'

The second man was yellow. He raised his hat politely, his hair was yellow too.

The first man said, 'Do you never seek to know what ails the world?'

'I hear educated guesses.'

'Snowballs in hell. He doesn't make His logic generally available.'

I said, 'If there's a reason why things are let happen I'd rather not know.'

'Knowledge is salvation. Deny it and you condemn yourself to everlasting fire.'

'The Lord saves!' cried the woman.

I said, 'I think ignorance is pardonable.'

'We are talking here about your immortal soul. There can be no quarter for the unbeliever.'

'Oh I like a good story. I know all the Old Testament ones. My mother packed me off to Sunday school so that she could be alone with Father Christmas. I didn't mind, I enjoyed the stories and during the preachy parts I made up my own. But you're right, gospel truth is something you have to work at. Ain't always liable what you read in the Bible.'

The yellow man shuffled his feet as if he was about to dance. The woman said sharply, 'We all got talents loaned us and got to account for what we done with them. How you going to account for yours?'

'I'll tell a story.'

'You may expect hell, madam,' said the white man. 'You may expect to fry along with the tares and the unclean organs of beasts.'

'Don't they make those into pet food?'

'There will be no suspended sentence, exculpation or pardon. You will burn for all eternity.'

'So that's settled. Thank you for calling.'

The woman put out a hand and stopped me closing the door. 'Lady, I had my purgatory in a handbag factory. Satan's own tricks played on me. They tied my overall sleeves, put matches in my tea, red-hot rivets on my chair and burned me to the buttock-bone. I'm unlucky with people, lucky with God.'

The yellow man stretched his neck and imitated a police siren.

'George,' the white man said sternly.

'What's he on about?' I said.

'The Word of the Lord.'

'It sounds more like an emergency.' The siren got louder and more insistent, the police car was coming right inside the porch. 'George, is there something you want to say?'

'There surely is,' said the woman. 'It takes him all his time.'

'Is he all right? He's yellow as a daffodil.'

'The Lord colours us black, brown, ruby-red, according to His plan. White He leaves so He can watch it darken.'

'Madam,' said the white man, 'insure your soul. Take out this policy of prayer—' he held up a pamphlet—'price fifty pence.'

The yellow man tried to kick his own feet from under him.

'Can he use your toilet?' the woman said urgently.

'I'm sorry—' the papers are full of the unwisdom of letting strangers into your house. 'There's a public convenience along the road.'

'Is fifty pence too high a premium for eternal life?'

'Oh no. Will you mind if I shut the door while I fetch my purse?'

But when I went back with the money they were hustling George through the gate.

IV

THERE ARE PLENTY of good apples but people are all specked. George Ruby was a borderline case, the way his speck developed he was incapable of committing a crime but capable of using the intent for his own advantage.

He had the reputation of being morose. His tongue had been tied in infancy by a loquacious mother. He could hardly get a whimper in edgeways. His father ran away, to another woman George's mother said. For years George believed that all women talked their heads off and that his father had gone for a change of subject.

When his mother died, she left him in a resounding silence, like the one after a box on the ears. In the house where they had lived for thirty years there remained a constant high-pitched whistling. It might have come from a working fridge, but it did not cease when George switched off the electricity. He assumed it was a sonic reaction, sound waves were still quivering.

He was sustained by scepticism during the funeral service. The mumbling of the clergy and the few mourners amused him because no one had been able to shut his mother up, certainly not in a box with brass handles.

It took time for him to accept that that fully operational jaw was stilled for ever. As an intimation of mortality it was food for thought. Thought was inhibiting. Thinking before he spoke, he tended to miss his turn, or by the time his turn came round, his contribution had been made by someone else.

It might be supposed that his job as a municipal parks attendant would give him opportunities to speak. But he presented a slow-moving target for anyone with time to spare, and he had been cautioned more than once by the

Parks Superintendent for gossipping when in fact he was waiting his turn.

Thinking of mortality, his conversational contributions seemed trifling, and with the idea of getting something worthwhile to say, he joined a drama group.

The Courtway Players were short of young males and the producer had hope of George. His figure was presentable although he needed to be shown how to carry himself. He wasn't bad-looking and might be made up to look better. The point at issue was the usual one: delivery.

'Try putting your shoulders back.' George tried. 'Head up!' Impatient, the producer chucked him under the chin.

'Hey,' said George.

'If you stand well it gives you presence. Pull your stomach in. Don't stick your neck out. Let me hear you speak.'

'It's my neck,' said George.

The producer picked up a book, opened it and handed it to him. 'Read.'

George moistened his lips. ' "How beautiful are thy feet with shoes—" ' He had pitched his voice too high and had to come down an octave. ' "The joints of thy thighs are like jewels." '

' "O prince's daughter." '

'Eh?'

'Continue.'

' "Thy joints are like jewels, the work of the hands of a cunning workman. Thy navel is like a round goblet, thy belly is like a heap of wheat set about with lilies." OK?'

' "Thy two breasts are like two young roes that are twins." It's magnificent, language at its greatest. Don't you feel that?'

'Huh,' said George.

'The Song of Songs is the finest love-poem of all time.'

'OK.'

George's first part was a watchman in an oldtime melodrama. He had a line to speak as he crossed the stage: 'It's twelve o'clock and all's well,' he enunciated with care, and brandished the Big Shopper which did duty as a lantern at rehearsals.

'Look,' said the producer, 'you wave a lantern about like that and you'll set the place alight. They were only wooden houses in those days, remember.'

George thought of saying he hadn't been around in those days. The producer, an irked man, made him do the scene over again. And again.

'Don't stomp—you're not on parade!'

George tried a Groucho Marx lope.

'Look,' said the producer, 'you're here to tell them they've got nothing to worry about and you're a bloody liar because they've got it all coming—the Black Death, the Fire of London, Women's Lib. But they don't know that. Nor do you. You sing to them, nice and tuneful, "Twelve o' the clock on a fine night and all's well".'

'I can't sing,' said George.

When they finally performed the play, George stood mid-stage, holding up his lantern as defiantly as any lollipop lady on a school crossing. He spoke his line loud and clear. Someone clapped. George bowed.

The Note on his mantelpiece next morning read: *I was proud of you last night*.

George was well satisfied. He had made a good beginning, spoken to an audience of several hundred people. Every night the play was performed he would speak to hundreds more.

But the producer was not pleased. 'Look, you don't take a curtain call in the middle of the first act. *You*—' he poked George in the chest—'don't take a solo curtain any time.'

George, looking, saw that to speak was one thing and to be understood was another.

'When we rehearse *Macbeth* I want you to be prompt,' said the producer. George, who was never late, felt offended. 'Read the play, get as much as you can by heart, with special attention to exits and entrances. We don't take liberties with the Bard. There's always someone ready to scream if we don't keep to the text. Ideally, prompt should know everybody's lines. I don't expect that of you, but I do expect you to know at all times what comes next. And to say it so that the actors can hear you and the audience can't. Think you can do it? We'll give it a try. I've got to see a girl about the bloody hands speech.' He bustled away, leaving George to think.

The Courtway Players' Lady Macbeth was the billion-and-oneth to play the part. She gave herself star-quality airs and picked fusses with the producer.

'Prompt—' she called to George, 'come and hear me speak my lines.' It was the first time she had addressed him directly. George stood before her, chewing his lip. 'Your name's Ruby, isn't it?'

'George Ruby.'

'I'll call you Ruby.' She was strong on diction and made it sound like a wine-gum. 'I'm called Liliane, the French way, with a long final vowel.' George thought of saying he didn't know any French. 'Names are important. If you've got the wrong one, you should change it. I did. I shan't tell you what mine was. But Ruby's right, Ruby's perfect for you.'

She put such feeling into her speeches that George began to wonder what he was missing. But it was the words which astonished him: hard, smooth, soft, dangerous, sweet, carney, rum, they dripped off her tongue. Like all virtuoso performances it was beyond understanding.

' "O proper stuff! This is the very painting of your fear: this is the air-drawn dagger which led you to Duncan. O, these flaws and starts—" ' She snapped her fingers. ' "Flaws and starts"—what comes after?'

George was thinking he couldn't cope with the acrobatics of feeling. He didn't know how to wring his hands, if he were to roll his eyes it would be jokey, and if he should try tearing his hair he would be left with a bald patch.

It was a safe bet that someone having so much to say

about murder would never do it. His own mother, who had not had a wide command of language and repeated herself ad nauseam, was no doer. She was fond of aphorisms and used strong lines like 'nothing venture, nothing gained, he who hesitates is lost'. George still worried about whether he should have his cake or eat it.

Murder, said Liliane Macbeth, giving it everything she had, except action. George thought that murder might be a talking point for him too.

'Ruby, you're not listening!'

He too could make dives at it. Lady M would have done it if the old man hadn't looked like her father. George didn't know what his father looked like, he could get away with murder.

'What's the matter? You deaf or something?'

'No,' said George.

'You're bloody useless!'

Something happened to him when she swore, a pang like an electric shock went through his loins. 'I was thinking.'

'What about?'

He wasn't ready to say, because that would have been throwing it away and he wanted to savour it. Even without the death penalty, putting an end to somebody was still the capital act. It could take a man out of the ordinary in one second flat, no specialisation required. George Ruby, parks attendant, rated a billion a penny. George Ruby, murderer, had to be of the greatest importance because so far no one had been able to get any farther than murder.

Coming to think of it, he seldom put an end to anything. He might finish a library book, a glass of beer, pools coupons, or hosing the conveniences in the Park and occasionally, in the line of duty, he had to finish off a few vermin. None of that was *stopped*, certainly not the vermin.

' "How now, my lord?" ' Liliane was off again. ' "Why do you keep alone, of sorriest fancies your companions making? Using those thoughts which should indeed have died with them they think on?" '

None of your business, he might have said.

'Ruby, you're a pig!'

Anger suited her. The colour came up under her skin like daylight, it was pretty to watch and George, watching, took credit for it.

His life was short on events. Other people had them; they fell and broke their legs, got caught shoplifting, had their cars clamped, went into hospital, married black girls. His legs were like tree trunks, stealing didn't turn him on, he rode a motor scooter and didn't know any blacks.

'You're a self-motivated shit,' said Liliane.

George was wondering about victims. Who to murder? He would prefer it not to be someone he knew intimately. But as he hadn't known anyone intimately since his mother, the field was open. Though not all that wide. There were people regularly encountered in the Park: the Parks Superintendent, acquaintances at the local, a woman who made sets at him in the washeteria, a cousin in Scarborough, the drama group—

'*Merde!*' said Liliane.

Alarmed, George stared. If she knew what he was going to say before he opened his mouth what was the use of saying anything?

At home he found a Note: *There's always Mrs Sandberg*.

Mrs Sandberg, his next-door neighbour, had come as close to him as she could get. 'You need never be alone,' she had said after his mother died, and she had brought her knitting and peppermints whenever she could catch him at home. She burped softly and continuously, patting her bosom and smiling roguishly. 'It's wind. We Sandbergs are liable to it.'

Then there was the question of committal. How should it be done? With a gun, a knife, a silk stocking? Where would he get a silk stocking?

It made a change to have serious problems. What he usually had to contend with were strayed children, flashers, wreckers, paddlers in the fishpond and humpers on the bowling-green. He supposed he should be glad about his sheltered life. Not that there was anyone to be grateful to. People said: 'It's all right for you, you're not married.' They also said that he didn't know he was born, which he resented.

Now that he had something to talk about, that people would listen to, there was bound to be a change. But only—this was where he scored—so far as he wanted a change. He was only going to be talking, and he could stop any time.

'George,' said the producer, 'I'm assuming you learned to read: "the cat sat on the mat, Mary had a little lamb", that kind of thing. Correct me if I'm wrong.'

'OK,' said George.

'And this kind of thing? "Be thou jocund: ere the bat hath flown his cloistered flight, ere to black Hecate's summons the shard-borne beetle with his drowsy hum, hath rung night's yawning peal, there shall be done a deed of dreadful note." '

'Sure,' said George.

'So what's he talking about?'

'Murder.'

The producer as victim did not appeal. The producer's heart was in the theatre, it left him no time for anything else, certainly not for being himself. He was a man without personality, impossible to be sure if he was good or bad. Or even if he was a good or bad producer.

A Note was propped on the mantelpiece: *There are twenty-thousand people in this borough, half of them malefactors.*

To which George replied, though not in so many words, that he wasn't prepared to sit in judgment, pass sentence and execute a criminal, he just wanted to put an end to someone special.

OK, OK—the Notes grew impatient—*that leaves a dozen possibilities.*

George sat in the Boar's Head and considered his drinking companions. Each was a man of character but each was married with a family and George wanted no widows and orphans on his conscience. And come closing time, there was nothing exclusive about any of them.

He couldn't see himself getting past Mrs Sandberg's indigestion with a stocking. Guns and knives were out he had decided: knives were messy, he had never handled a gun and anyway he hadn't a licence.

You know who—what are you waiting for?

'The right moment,' said George, and screwed up the Note.

It might be thought that the blood and thunder they were rehearsing pre-empted the moment. On the other hand, the real thing would come realer. George Ruby talking about murder could make Macbeth sound as significant as a bowl of Rice Crispies.

'Now,' said the producer, 'the news you've been waiting for. We're going to do Restoration comedy for the Festival.'

'What, no more murder?' Someone took the words out of George's mouth.

'One gunshot in the second act.'

'In Restoration comedy?'

'This is a modern version.' There was a general groan. 'The gun's just a bit of fun. This is a very important production. We're going for the County Drama Award. We'll be facing strong competition.'

'The police pantomime!'

'This will be a team effort, everybody taking part.'

'What about Ruby?' said Liliane.

'Him too.'

'Non-speaking?'

'George has a good speaking voice, he only needs to be taught how to use it.'

George had to smile. Because he had nothing to say, people thought there was something wrong with his throat. 'Get yourself some Fisherman's Friends,' Mrs Sandberg had told him, 'lubricate your vocal chords.'

He was going to show them that he could use his voice, they were in for a surprise, and Liliane was in for the biggest.

She was smiling at him, half-shutting her eyes as if she was reckoning up his collar size. George smiled back, he felt they were in private communication.

She came and sat beside him, swinging her knees round so that one was touching his. 'Don't let them get to you, Ruby. You're the only man I've ever met who doesn't talk. It makes you unique. Remember that. Everyone else is gassing away, polluting the atmosphere. Lead in petrol, nuclear waste is nothing to what we do to the air with our own breath.'

George couldn't make out whether she was serious. She was smiling, but what she said wasn't comical. 'I can talk,' he said.

'But you don't, and that's such a relief.' She removed her knee. The pressure of it had been largely responsible for his not taking in what she was saying. Before she walked away, she put her forefinger to her lips. It might have been an injunction to silence, it might have been the sign of a kiss.

"'Tis pity she's a whore," said someone.

George stood up, glaring. There was a general titter.

'It's just a bit of Restoration fun, old chap.'

'Hardly,' said the producer tartly. 'Well, that's all for tonight. We'll be casting next week.'

When Liliane left the hall, George followed her. He was experiencing an emotional state, his stomach took deep psychological dives, the backs of his knees sweated. His mouth was bone-dry. He sucked in his cheeks and licked his lips to get up some juice.

Liliane walked fast with a short compact gait. Her heels tick-tocked on the pavement, sounding important. George floundered behind, keeping her in sight. If she turned and saw him it would be finish. He couldn't utter in this busy street. What he had to say would be lost under the buses.

Not that he knew yet what words he would use, or how many. But it would come right once he started.

'I can talk,' he said to Liliane's back.

She turned a corner into a short street with a warehouse on one side and a dairy depot on the other. A man was hosing the milk floats and the sweetish smell of milk stirred George strangely.

He sprang, and in one easy movement landed on the balls of his feet behind Liliane's shoulder. Something, his shoes or his bones, creaked. She swung round.

'Get away! Why—Ruby, it's you!' He stood with his hands upheld, enclosing as much space as he thought her neck would take. It was a plump neck and he opened his hands wider. 'What on earth are you doing?'

'I'm going to strangle you.' There spoke George Ruby, murderer.

Immediately she laughed, without a minute to take it in, be shocked, alarmed, she laughed a ringing stage laugh which caused the man washing the milk floats to look in their direction.

'Is that the worst you can do to me?'

Turning away, she touched her fingers to her lips. This time there was no doubt, she was blowing him a kiss.

A Note was waiting for George at home: *There's always you.*

It was stating the obvious, but the Notes always made a point which hadn't been made before. He puzzled for days before it dawned on him, slow and chilling.

Suicide hadn't crossed his mind, he hadn't any problems big enough to merit it. Now, suddenly, here was a nod more than a wink, something larger than life stooped close and froze his natural assets. With less thought he might have ignored it—he could hardly be blamed. But since he had got the message he was morally and legally bound—the Notes were always moral and legal—to keep on thinking about it.

He gave it some unproductive thought. The bottom had fallen out of murder and self-murder wasn't a conversational gambit. For a start, he couldn't supply the in-depth analysis.

George saw that it was a case of not being able to have his cake and eat it. He got depressed, neglected his Park, spoke only in monosyllables and only when spoken to.

Of course no one noticed or was concerned, until the night of the County Festival production. George was required to come on stage, fire a pistol into the air, and exit. Instead, he put the gun to his head, pulled the trigger and fell flat on his back when the cap exploded.

Those on stage stood paralysed, the curtain jammed, the audience sat waiting. After a full minute's hush, the producer rushed on and dragged George's body out by the feet. In the wings someone—not Liliane—tried to give George the kiss of life. George sat up, indignant. The actors on stage exited in confusion and the audience started a slow clap.

The producer hauled George up by his coat collar and ran him out of the theatre. He swore that if George came near the Courtway Players again he would personally shoot him for real.

George walked away on air, happy, free, and his own man. In the Boar's Head he called for a pint of bitter. The Note on the beer mat said: *You did it!*

*

Angie should hear about another of my facets. 'At night when I can't sleep I look at the pictures in our art gallery.'

In the night? she says.

'The pictures that talk to me I stand in front of and study till I can recall them in detail, right down to the brush strokes. I'm good at brush strokes. I could have been a painter.'

She says what a loss it would have been to my audience.

The gallery is in the old mansion in the Park which was once a gentleman's estate. The last occupier was a biscuit baron, he made the estate over to the borough council for the benefit of local residents. The gate with his family crest and a Latin inscription: *Si sic omnia*, which I translate as 'everyone's so fed up', have been incorporated into municipal railings. I can still smell custard creams in the house.

He was a collector of pictures in a random way. They hang on the walls, some originals, some reproductions and a lot of Victoriana. The originals range from watercolours of dignified boats on quilted seas, and raging blobs which resolve into a scene, any scene, if you look long enough. The prints are rather risky, they have titles like 'Betrothed', 'Wedded', 'The Tryst'. The reproductions are of master works. I go and look at the Rembrandts on my way to Sainsbury's.

This morning I was looking at that portrait of Saskia as the goddess of spring. She is holding her dress over her stomach, either a big stomach or a big dress. She might be pregnant. She has flowers on her head, they don't look too fresh, and in her hand a sort of kebab of flowers on a stick. She looks tipsy.

What did she think when she looked at the picture? She had to be comfortable if she was to give him comfort, which was her purpose in life. His was to paint, and he painted her dipped in himself. I saw him as Charles Laughton once and *he* looked a barfly.

'God, there she is!'

'Where?'

'In that picture, wearing breast plates and waving a spear.'

'It's called "The Warrior Queen".'

'It's her, the female eunuch.'

I looked round. They were concentrating on a picture on the far wall. I don't think they registered I was there, let alone listening.

'She's always been kind to me.'

'Kind's easy. Especially to you.'

'So what happened?'

'I'd organised it so she wouldn't be there, I'd left her a note, it was all settled, and she had to come in as I was bringing my bags downstairs. I'm going, I said, straight out, for good, I said, so there'd be no mistake. She knew, she said. How could she know, I said. It was a reasonable assumption, she said, judging by the amount of luggage I was taking.'

'What did you say?'

'What could I say? I said goodbye. She didn't answer. That's how she is, cold as a fish, all remote control.'

The man put his arms round the girl and they kissed.

V

ELINOR DUNPHY—elegant, gifted, remotely controlled, but passionate. Passion she must have had: being a reasonable woman, she kept it for her art. She was an artist, a water-colourist, designed Christmas and special occasion cards, was in demand for that. She did fragile, puzzling collages with whatever came to hand and mind. Most successful and least puzzling was her Eiffel Tower made of bloater bones.

She lived in a sweetly pretty mews cottage which no longer smelled of horses. It was pink-washed walls, cotton-tuft rugs and Korean basketry for Elinor. To look at her—slender, elegant, gifted—you would expect her never to get any nastier than the exquisite watercolour of Fly Agaric, a scarlet toadstool with white polka dots which she did for a Child's Guide to Poisonous Fungi. And you would suppose she came no closer to earth than the nylon rabbit on her pillow.

She had friends, some of whom were close enough to call her Ellie, which didn't suit her, and Dumpy, which she was not. With a few men closeness became demonstrable. She reserved her own demonstrations for her drawings, so the affairs were one-sided. As there was no good reason, like money, for a man to throw himself away, Elinor's suitors soon stopped suiting. Some were reticent about it, others openly annoyed. The charitable conclusion was that Elinor was hard to please: the uncharitable that she was sexless. Icebergia Preciosa one man, a market-gardener, called her.

She was asked to parties. Sipping gin and French, holding her glass as if it was a burstable bubble, slanting her slender neck over chicken marengo, she was a decorative element. She was the right shape, had a bloom on her skin, gloss on her hair, sinuosity and bodily fragrance. She appeared to be an eminently desirable woman if only somebody could sustain his desire in face of her lack of it.

Hers was a temperate nature. Such desire as she had was for perfection. Every robin's feather, every petal of every flower on her greetings cards had to be just right, every verse apposite, every sentiment heart-stirring. Humble she was not. She took pleasure in her work. It paid badly but was unfailingly well-intentioned, which is something nowadays. And while everybody else was writing books, painting landscapes and appearing on television, there had to be less than one in a million designing special occasion cards. Nowadays, Elinor reasoned, that was exclusivity.

When she was asked to an anti-grouse-shooting party she went in the expectation of encountering a few cranks. It was a pity, she thought, that the people who had the right ideas should hold them so clumsily. Having pinned on her lapel a diamanté brooch in the form of an arrow, she removed it as inconsiderate.

She always tried to consider other people's feelings, tastes and compulsions. She would not herself harm any living creature, and actually talked to and comforted worms, moths and woodlice as she rescued them from unpromising situations. But she had to accept that there were people who had a compulsion to kill, to put an end to life—a process which they themselves could set in motion but could never fully comprehend. She reasoned that it was an admission of defeat and a declaration of dismay. Reason took her no farther, reason assured her that she had neither the ability nor the inclination to sit in judgment. Besides, it was easier not to.

The kind of cranks likely to go to the Grossmiths' party cared only intermittently about grouse being shot. The Grossmiths had a well-earned reputation as party-givers. Madge Grossmith produced heavenly food and Arnold was a wine buff. This occasion amounted to cajolement, if not bribery, because their daughter Agnes was in earnest about the grouse. She wanted them declared a protected species.

Elinor said gently, 'I hardly think there's much hope of that.'

'Oh I know!' cried Madge. 'But the poor darling takes it to heart. We can't bear to see her suffer.'

Agnes was their only child and every breath she drew was sacred to her parents.

Elinor sighed. 'She's right of course. They shouldn't be hunted for sport. Such an ambiguous word, don't you think?'

'What word?'

'Sport. It means running, jumping, racing, swimming, playing ball, having fun. And killing.'

'We have tried to talk to her.'

'It also means a deviation from the norm.'

'Agnes is perfectly normal!'

'Of course she is. A normal teenager.' Elinor's smile was sweet. 'Normal teenagers are overly sensitive.'

'People can be so thoughtless!'

'I suppose shooting to kill requires some basic, technical thought. Ultimately it is unthinking and unthinkable.'

'I mean in what they *say*. Agnes gets so upset. Oh you wouldn't, of course—' Madge, floundering, looked at Elinor with the eyes of a poor swimmer, 'you wouldn't say anything to upset her, you're so thoughtful—'

'Who's that talking to her now?'

'Edgar Allan Poe.'

'What?'

Madge's lip trembled. 'He says there's no copyright in names.'

Elinor laughed, a silvery cadence which caused heads to turn, among them Agnes Grossmith's and Edgar Allan Poe's.

Agnes came over, a blanched girl, herself at risk. One could see the risk in the watery eye, the bitten fingernails and—it was most unfortunate, something she could have been cured of—her habit of licking her lips.

She addressed Elinor after lubrication. 'Are you coming to the demo?'

'Demo?' Madge cried. 'What demo?'

'There's got to be one.' Agnes frowned at Elinor. 'That's why we're here, to organise it.'

Elinor doubted that. There were people directly in her line of vision who would have come only for Madge's Coquilles St Jacques and Arnold's Chateau Richesse. 'Of course I'll help any way I can.'

'Agnes, darling, please don't get involved in any violence.' Madge appealed to Elinor. 'We have to be careful, she's not strong, she so easily becomes hyperactive—'

'Violence!' cried Agnes, also to Elinor. 'Do you have any idea of the violence done to those birds? They *beat* them out of cover, men—grown men waving flags drive them on to the guns—'

'It's unsporting,' agreed Elinor.

'The birds are made to fly into the wind and at the last moment, as they turn away from the guns they're shot down. In the season hundreds, thousands of birds are left dead and dying. It's a bloody massacre!'

Madge moaned and Elinor said 'I believe the grouse—' and thinking to introduce a little light relief— 'why don't we call them grice?—I believe they're very fast on the wing.'

'So?' said Agnes.

'Only a first-class shot—and there can't be so many of those—can score a . . . hit.' Elinor, hoping to minimise matters was aware that she had made it sound like a coconut shy. Agnes gave her a sickened stare and turned away.

'Oh dear,' mourned Madge.

'You shouldn't worry unduly. Agnes is a sensible girl.' That word, too, had more than one meaning.

'She gets carried away.'

'Is there anyone here to carry her away?'

'What? Oh—perhaps not.'

They both looked at a woman diametrically opposite, wearing a mauve crimplene trouser-suit. Both smiled, then something happened at their side. Elinor was aware of a disparity, a sudden imbalance of air, or emotion. She herself wasn't experiencing any specific emotion at that moment, but Madge was. They both looked round.

Elinor got a profound shock. Again, she couldn't see a reason for it or, at any rate, for the profundity of it. A young man with the regulation Rossetti hair-shower and bomber jacket stood beside them. He was good-looking in a plain way and reminded Elinor of a medieval painting of St Sebastian complacently receiving flights of arrows in his well-fleshed stomach. It could only be the association which alarmed her, she was alerted but not scared.

'Oh dear.' There was nothing obscure about Madge's helplessness. 'This is Agnes's friend Edgar.' The young man held out his hand. Elinor, not taking it, gestured with her glass, whereupon he shook hands with himself. 'Elinor is our artist,' said Madge.

Elinor winced at the 'our'. The young man bowed over his joined hands in an Oriental manner.

'Poe, at your service.'

'I must go and see about the canapés,' said Madge. Elinor, tight-lipped, watched her swim away with a feeble breast stroke, touching people as she passed.

'Funny lady,' said the young man. Elinor looked at him with eyebrows arched, he at her with serenity. Po-faced, thought Elinor, and felt a little happier. 'So you're the artist.'

'An.'

'Pleased to know you, Ann.'

Again he held out his hand and again Elinor did not take it. 'I am *an* artist.'

This time he did not shake hands with himself. He turned his out-stretched arm slowly, rigidly, until his hand was palm up and his arm trembled with effort. Elinor saw what had alerted her. The complacency, tranquillity, piousness, was a blanket-cover, wool over iron, fire, bad temper. 'What do you paint?'

'Everything.' She added, to try him, 'I once did a colophon for a special edition of *The Fall of the House of Usher*.'

'I've seen one of those in a jar.'

'I beg your pardon?'

'A colophon. It was alive, it had two heads.' Elinor turned away. 'Hey, don't go!'

Elinor went, and passing Agnes Grossmith heard her declare to the managing director of a firm which advertised in *The Field*, 'We must show fight!'

It was pathetic, as Elinor would have said had there been someone to say it to. She left it unsaid rather than get into the habit of talking to herself.

She found that she was making provision for something, with a degree of disquiet. It vexed her: how foolish when she was not even sure how much, or what, she had to fear! Did she go so far as to fear? She frowned at her face in the mirror.

The truth was she had picked up some sort of warning from the man calling himself Edgar Allan Poe, and whatever it was had already started.

Ridiculous, she told herself. It was merely a transient impression of an unprepossessing person. Leaving her drawing board, she went in search of grasses, flowers, berries and acorn cups. She needed specimens for her Mothers' Day series.

There had been a lot of rain, on the paths were hundreds of wormlets, pink and white and tender. Some had been trodden on and dissolved into milkiness. All were dead. She saw a hedgehog which had been run over and was nastier.

The next day was Sunday. She succumbed to an outdated superstition and went to church. If people were surprised to see her there, only the vicar was unmannerly enough to say so. He saluted her with billowing surplice.

'How nice! May we hope to see you again at divine service?'

Elinor, who had somehow derived confidence from the smell of the hymnals, supposed he was including God in the hope, and said they could. Hope, she meant, but the vicar took it for a firm promise and called a breezy 'au revoir' as she went through the churchyard.

She arrived home with the intention of washing her hair. She had long hair braided in a knot at the nape of her neck and was in the habit of washing it in the kitchen sink because the bathroom basin was too small to accommodate the quantity of water she needed—rainwater heated on the stove. It was an undertaking which, once embarked on, she felt would effectively stop anything else happening. She was unreasonable enough to put her faith in that.

He arrived as she was starting the final rinse. She saw his fringed jeans out of the corner of her eye, confirmation of what she already knew. Sight unseen, she had sensed his presence and knew that he had got in through the kitchen door which would have kept him out had she remembered to lock it, the fundamental point being that she had forgotten with what she now suspected was a degree of deliberation.

This flashed damagingly through her mind as he took the pan of warmed rainwater from the stove and with the fingers of his free hand gently lifted and swilled strands of hair while he poured the water over her head.

What could she say, except thank you? All else, his entering though not breaking, was fait accompli. He had known that it would happen.

She wrapped her hair in a towel, twisted the towel turbanwise, and tucked in the ends. When she turned to look at him a trickle of water ran down her cheek.

She meant to be as calm as he was. That Edgar Allan Poeface was too much, *he* was too much. She had better be careful. 'What are you doing here?' There was no harm in asking but she had better not be serious.

'Clothes do this.'
'Do what?'
'Change people. You are now a princess.'
'Because I've got a towel round my head?'
'Where's your husband?'
'Upstairs.'
'In bed, waiting for you?'
'I'd like you to go.'
'You haven't got a husband. Agnes said so.'
'So why did you ask?'
'Why did you lie?'

Elinor considered pretending that there was someone, a lover, upstairs, but this man was capable of going up to check. She wouldn't be able to stop him. It occurred to her that she wouldn't be able to stop whatever he chose to do.

People had told Elinor that her house was isolated, that she should get a dog, a burglar alarm, a hot line to the police station, because one day something could happen.

She sighed. Regret at this juncture was futile, an element of wistfulness was significant. What of? And since when had she needed to analyse her reactions? The answer must be that she was experiencing a slight physical dysfunction of some organ or organs unknown.

She unwound the towel, shook her hair free, and rubbed it. 'Why have you come?'

'To tell you about the demo. It's at ten o'clock on Tuesday at the Salt Box. That's where they meet. We'll start on the cars.'

'Start?'

'Put stickers on them, tell them what to expect. Will you come?'

'I have to go to London on Tuesday.'

'You have lovely hair, lovely clean hair. God, I hate dirt!' Elinor looked at his feet in their muddy sneakers. 'Here,' he whipped away the towel, cracked it like a window-cleaner's leather and twisted it round his hands. 'Let me.'

Elinor drew back. 'I prefer to dry my own hair.'

'Suit yourself.'

He tossed the towel to her and walked away along the passage to the sitting room. She had no choice but to follow. She wanted to call out but was prevented by the problem of what to call: 'Stop Poe—Poe come back—Edgar Allan, will you please leave my house!' It was unfunny. In fact, the name was probably intended, like everything about him, to obstruct, obscure and off-load.

She found him standing in the middle of her sitting room. His back was towards her, his knuckles lightly resting on his hips. He was looking round.

She threw back her wet rope of hair. 'I don't remember inviting you and I'm busy. I'd like you to go.'

'I don't see your work.'

'I'm in the midst of washing my hair!'

'Where are your pictures?' He was pushing open the door into what had been the cottage parlour and was now her studio.

It was the ultimate effrontery. Her work, besides being her livelihood, was her second nature, and immeasurably the better of the two: nicer, happier. She thought, when she had done something especially good, that she had found a way of having her cake and eating it. Real artists feel like that.

She rarely let anyone into her studio: this man she would have taken steps to keep out—like locking the door, all the doors, shutting the windows. She had an uncalled-for vision, a pen and ink drawing of herself as a demented stick-woman, hair raying out as she ran through the house barricading it. Against Edgar Allan Poe. It was another warning. Without even trying, he could make a fool of her. She should be very careful, anger was no help.

'This it?' After a cursory glance round, he turned to her, he wasn't prepared to spend time on it if it wasn't.

'This is where I work.'

He contemplated her, nodding as if at some trite disclosure which only he could hear.

'My head's cold,' Elinor said, and started massaging her scalp with her fingertips. At all costs she must keep her temper.

He moved about the room, stooping to look, but not touching she was relieved to see. There was something high-shouldered about him, expressive of distaste. 'Where are your paintings?'

'I do watercolours and line-drawings mostly. For special occasion cards—Christmas, birthdays.'

'What's special about getting older?'

Elinor had wondered that too. 'A lot of people think that being born is cause for celebration.'

For the first time she heard him laugh. 'You'll come to the demo?'

'I've already said I have to go to London.'

'Come, for my sake.'

'Do you care so much about the grouse?'

'No. It's those people shouting and tramping I care about, shouting and tramping over one, they're not human, they're God, God-in-boots.'

'Really?' It manifestly wasn't, and Elinor felt there was a catch coming up.

'One hides, one goes to ground, down a hole or a drainpipe or in a bottle—that colophon was dying in the bottle—you could die and be glad to, but they won't let you. They beat you out, they beat on the drainpipe till the noise drives you crazy and you rush out and they let you have it with both barrels.'

Elinor, looking for the catch, was caught in an immensity in his eyes, like the endless sequence of opposing mirrors.

'You must come!'

He went, leaving her with a sense of chill which she blamed on her damp hair.

Madge Grossmith ran her trolley into Elinor's heels in the supermarket. Madge was in trouble as usual, the usual trouble—her daughter Agnes.

'Have you heard what happened?'

'That depends on the happening.'

Elinor alienated people by her manner. It was often intentional, she found so many people put-downable. But it took more than a manner to put Madge down.

'Tuesday—at the Salt Box!'

'Ah, the demo. Were you there?'

'No, I had a migraine. But Agnes—oh we tried to stop her!—and a crowd of young people—I don't know who they were or where they came from—'

'And Poe?'

'What?'

'Edgar Allan. Was he there?'

'He interceded with the police.'

'Police?'

'Elinor, it's so awful! Apparently everything was quiet and orderly at first, just people walking round with placards and handing out leaflets. Then these hooligans, vandals, turned up and threw paint over the cars. Somebody rang the police, but of course they'd gone by the time the police arrived. All except Agnes. She told the police that her supporters—supporters mind you!—lacked the courage of their convictions. She was taken into custody, charged with riotous conduct—'

'And Edgar Allan Poe—did he run away?'

'No, he wasn't involved. Apparently. He tried to help Agnes, talked to the police—'

'What did he say?'

'He said she hadn't actually done any of the damage, she hadn't meant any harm, she was simply making a protest against a barbarous sport, when things got out of hand. We shall have to pay for the damage and the police will bring charges.'

'You've spoken to them of course?'

'Do you know—they asked if Agnes was of diminished responsibility!'

'Aren't we all?' Elinor laid a soothing hand on Madge's cornflakes. 'Try not to worry, it will blow over. Agnes has sufficient sense to let it be a lesson to her.' Privately, Elinor was of the opinion that Agnes Grossmith suffered from the combined shortcomings of both her parents.

'They'll take her fingerprints, photograph her, put her on their files—she'll have a criminal record!' Weeping, Madge took up a deep-frozen chicken and dropped it into her trolley. 'The things they asked!'

'What sort of things?'

'About Arnold's business, his position in the firm, whether he has a company car—' Madge blanched— 'intimate details of our personal relationships, Arnold's and mine—and Agnes's. We have nothing to be ashamed of, but they made us feel ashamed.'

Elinor dislodged the frozen chicken from one of Mr Kipling's excellent fruit pies and said she thought the police ought to question Mr Poe.

She was to assume, later, that they did. It was one of her assumptions about him which was wrong and could have been dangerous. Any reasonable assumption about him could be dangerous. She was curled up on the windowseat in the sunniest corner of her studio, making inspired strokes on her drawing board. Her first strokes were always the best, they showed genius which she knew she had, but could not sustain. One day she would sustain it, meanwhile she had to be content with capability and was, most of the time. But it was a delight to see her brush travelling boldly, independent of conscious craft. There was divinity in it, and a sublime joy, something she had never experienced in church, she was glad to say: glad, because it was unassisted and exclusive. She was naturally exclusive, congregations diminished her.

The young man stood outside her window and scratched the pane to be let in. Elinor opened the casement. 'You again?'

More than anything she disliked the ambivalence of her feelings. Here she was, two parts angry, one part glad to see him. As he leaned across the sill the stubble on his cheek glinted gold. Mrs Poe's boy, she reminded herself.

'Help.' He spoke quietly, as if the word came into a conversation they were already having.

'Try the door.'

'Help me.'

'I don't encourage people to enter my house by the window.'

'Don't talk like that!'

There was deep hurt in his voice. She found it gratifying, which had to be because she disliked him.

'I've just had the windowseat recovered so I expect I shall talk like that to anyone who proposes to walk on it.'

'Like a premeditated bitch. I know you're not. I shan't touch anything. Stand back.'

She had no time to guess his intention. He sprang through the open window with one beautifully collected leap. One second she saw him poised in mid-air, the next he was at her side and was steadying a pot of dried grasses teetering on the sill.

Words failed Elinor, besieged—breached—in her own home. She considered this young man who unnerved and compelled her. The unnerving she thought was due to the generation gap, realising how removed—advanced or retarded, whichever way one liked to look at it—younger people were nowadays. The compulsion was her own, and she couldn't blame him for that. Nor could she say whether it came from her heart or her head, which was putting it nicely. Wry-lipped, she laid down her brush.

'What's that you're painting?'

'A mandrake root.'

'It's dead ugly.'

'I'm designing a logo for a credit card.'

'What's a root got to do with credit?'

'Isn't money the root of all evil? The mandrake has a bad reputation. They won't let me use it, of course.'

'You like painting ugly things?'

'It's just a bit of fun.'

'Will you paint for me?'

He dropped to the floor and sat on his heels looking up

at her, teasing, she thought. 'Do you think painting is something I can sit down and do for your entertainment? Like playing the piano?'

'Paint *me*. I'll pay anything you ask. A hundred, a thousand pounds!'

'Don't be ridiculous.'

'I'm uglier than that root.'

'I don't paint portraits.'

'Not the outside, the inside. What's going on. Show me to me, I need to see, I need to know.'

'I suggest you go to a doctor.'

'It's all happening inside me!'

'That's the general principle. But if you think about it, it becomes oppressive.' He produced a pack of cigarettes, struggled with shaking hand, to light one. She said soothingly, 'The whole process is meant to operate with the minimum of cooperation from you.'

'You think they let me think? They don't even let me *be*!' He walked about, stabbing the air with the lit cigarette. 'It's do this, do that, why aren't you, where are you, who are you?'

'I'd rather you didn't smoke.'

'Who's anyone anyway? Who the hell are *they*?'

'They're doing their job and you'd be advised to stay on their right side.'

'They don't have a right side!'

'The police are a moral force, however misguided they sometimes seem.'

'Police? I'm talking about devils in hell!'

Elinor worried about the sparks as he brandished his cigarette. 'Please put that out.'

He stood still. She recognised the violence, it had been there all the time, under his skin that looked so thick and was so terribly thin.

'Christ, I hate cigarettes!' He snatched them one by one from the pack, breaking each in half.

'There's no need for that—'

'Oh there's *need*.' He scattered the pieces. 'You're the

only one who can help me. You can paint them out, get them down on paper—black, red, green. Green's the worst, that's the woman, she starts by mothering me: eat your breakfast, change your socks, get a regular girl, go and wash, wash between your legs, you don't want to smell like a man. She tells me I'm not a man, I'm not real, I leaked out before my mother was ready. I'm flux!'

Elinor said mechanically, 'How absurd.'

'And the black keeps nag-nagging.'

'The black?'

'The black voice. About how my insides are deteriorating, because after twenty-one you stop growing and start dying. It won't let me forget: your ticker missed a tick just then, didn't you feel it? You're running down, who's going to wind you up? Your arteries are hardening, your blood's not getting through, if it doesn't get through to your brain you end up cabbage.'

'You're being morbid.'

'If they let me alone I'd be OK, happy ever after. Then there's the red voice. It tells me what to do, it shouts, cracks my eardrums.'

'What does it tell you to do?'

He flung himself over a chair, somehow managed to reach under the seat and grab his ankles. 'I never remember, it goes in one ear and out the other.'

'We all have ideas which we don't—we couldn't—act upon.'

'I will! I'll act if you don't stop me!'

Bent backward across the chair, hands to feet, he reminded Elinor of a picture she had seen of Isaac bound for the sacrifice. 'Do get up, you're being ridiculous.' She was thinking that he had adopted this contorted position to plug his helplessness, which was something she did not believe in.

He closed his eyes, tensed himself. A spasm lifted him clear of the chair. His body arched, blood trickled from his mouth.

Elinor supposed he was having some sort of fit. She

could not bring herself to touch him. The way his body strained and shook was sick. And erotic. She felt faint and reached for the back of the chair for support. Immediately her fingers touched the chair, he relaxed, sank into it as fast as a pan of milk snatched off the boil.

Then he stood up with one easy movement, looking into her face and wiping his bitten lip on the back of his hand.

He went without another word. Elinor started to gather up the broken cigarettes and on an impulse, lit one. She had never smoked, but she had some notion of coming to terms with the encounter. The terms had to be her own, she was past terminology, in fact she had started at a point on the far side of it.

The cigarette smoke tasted like burned sacking. Or hell. She did not believe in hell, but Edgar Allan did. She plunged the lighted cigarette into her water jar.

One did not catch madness like a cold.

The mandrake root had ceased to amuse. She put it away in a cupboard. The credit card logo could wait, the Mothers' Day cards must have priority.

She found difficulty in settling to work. It was not unknown, there were times when the drawing board was not enough. She might be working on cards for Christmas and suddenly see past a spray of winter aconite to the winter beyond.

This time she experienced actual unwillingness to sit down at her drawing board. She moved around the house, finding chores. Stood at the window, watching.

She supposed she was tired and needing a holiday. A reasonable supposition, she had worked all summer without a break. What she felt now was physical disquiet, and completely unproductive. She put down her duster. There was no problem about the designs, she knew the sort of thing that was wanted. Getting it on paper would be at least as straightforward as dusting. Words too: when had she ever had trouble with the words? Years, tears, fear, dear, sorrows, tomorrows, true, you, laughter, after—she could string them like beads.

She had finished half a dozen roughs by lunchtime. She bundled them into her portfolio and took the afternoon train to town. I must get away she said aloud as the two-thirty to Waterloo ran shrieking into a tunnel and nobody could hear her.

'I wonder,' she said, while Lamplugh, her publisher, was looking at the sketches, 'could I ask you for an advance?' She was thinking that if the advance was generous she would book a package to Majorca, and if it wasn't she would go to Bournemouth.

Lamplugh, who had several times tried to be more to her than her publisher, shovelled the sketches together. 'You can ask, girlie, but you won't get.'

'No?'

'Not for these. They're no use to me. Lambs, kittens, bindweed—'

'Bryony.'

'Lambs equate to sheep, kittens to cats, and I know bindweed when I see it. Unfortunate associations. What were you thinking of?'

'Young creatures, clinging plants, what motherhood's about.'

'I'm surprised at you. Where did you get the verses? From a baby-pants commercial?'

'I'm sorry if you don't—'

'You ever been a mother, Elinor?'

'Are you making it a condition of my employment?'

'I wouldn't go as far as that. Motherhood's a splendid situation and requires special understanding to appreciate what it means.'

'No more than it takes to appreciate what it means to be a Christmas tree or an Easter egg.'

She picked up her portfolio and let herself out.

She wasn't going to be able to get away after all. But she was surprised at how far she had already got. It was as if days had passed since she left home. The days had passed over, she thought with a pang. Looking through the train window she thought that the landscape had been set up for something, was privately possessed. How intent it all was. *Aimed*, she thought. The fact was—she must try to hold on to facts—she hadn't wanted to come home. She had taken against her own place, had there been somewhere else for her to go she would have gone.

'How ridiculous!' This time a woman sitting opposite heard and eyed her with suspicion. Elinor said fiercely, 'I refuse to be intimidated!' and the woman glanced up at the emergency cord. Elinor felt stronger.

It was raining heavily when she got out of the train. She would have taken a taxi but was mindful of the fact that she hadn't been paid. She walked.

He was waiting for her. Another fact—really the only one she had to contend with. Vowing to contend it, she walked right past where he sheltered under her walnut tree.

He followed, of course. She could not quite bring herself to shut the door in his face. She went through to the kitchen to take off her wet things. He came and watched from the doorway as she shook out her coat.

'I don't like kitchens. They smell of death.' Elinor turned to look at him. His clothes were heavily stained with damp. Obviously he had remained in the same spot under the tree, not bothering to move when the rain leaked through. 'They smell of burned flesh.'

Here we go, she thought. 'I'm in no mood for this sort of thing.'

'What sort of thing?'

'Hell and damnation.'

'I'm thinking about hot dinners, all the animals you've roasted.'

'I think you've got into bad thinking habits and the sooner you drop them the better.'

'I'm trying to, that's why I'm here.'

'I have wondered why you're here.'

'You must help me.'

'I'm sorry, I don't wish to hear any more.'

He fell to his knees in front of her, as if to beg. She made to step back, he seized and held her feet.

'Listen! You've got to. You're the only one who can help me.'

Elinor was conscious of her feet, the consciousness was mounting up her legs. 'Please let me go!'

His fingers tightened. 'Just listen. They're bombing, burning and tearing me apart, twenty-eight, thirty hours out of the twenty-four. They fix the clock, they can fix anything.'

'They?'

'How would you like the whole bloody shoot in 3D on your eyelids? Plugged into your eardrums, up your nose? So you can't shut it out, you can't get away!'

Elinor, clutching at his shirt, smelt the close damp smell of the wool. It made her head swim. 'I don't know what you're talking about.'

'Listen, get their pictures, get them down on paper, get them out of me! Draw them!'

'Draw what?'

'The voices. Be sure and draw them green as grass and red as blood and black as hell.'

His hands moved up her legs. Elinor beat at his shoulders. 'Let me go!'

He did, suddenly, so that she almost fell. 'Tomorrow, I'll come back tomorrow.' And was gone, with a violence that left the room swinging round her.

She sank into a chair. She was near to tears, and what in heaven's name was there to cry about?

As a reasonable woman she accepted that there must be a reason. One which did not bear looking into. It was sick, answering to his sickness. If she fell back on terminology—psychotic, neurotic, manic-depressive—where would it leave her? Not nearly low enough. She was honest as well as reasonable.

As there was nothing else to do, nobody to tell it to— who in the world could she tell *that* to?—she went to her drawing board. There were still the Mothers' Day cards to get right. She could forget herself in her work, she was pretty desperate to forget.

When she picked up her pencil she was thinking of a woman in a floral pinafore crumbling suet into a basin: her own mother, just about the safest thought she could have. And as usual, when the pencil touched the block, it went its own way. She never knew where it would take her, but it could be relied upon to pick up her theme and give it a slant. Those first lines were inspiration, the rest was craft, know-how, commercial art, and no less enjoyable. The first lines were the purest joy.

She watched to see what her pencil would do. It drew a hand, in the hand a flower. Then she saw that the flower was a spike and it was through the hand.

She sat staring at it. Then she tore the top sheet off the block, crumpled it into a ball and gave herself a large whisky.

Daylight was fading. She decided to eat supper and go to bed. An unwise decision. She lay wide awake, her eyes ached with staring. She hadn't realised there were so many colours in the dark. She saw blue, yellow, green, gold, purple, thermal pink. Black, she thought, is compound, and switched on the light.

She went to her studio. She was thinking black is the end of the rainbow as she picked up her sketching block and started to draw.

This time her pencil drew a heart, the good old commercial shape, a shield with a nick in the top. At least it was appropriate to Mothers' Day. Anatomically it was near enough. She had seen ox hearts, big blue pear-shaped things. Offal was the dismissive name for the chief vital part, the circulator of blood, the seat of love.

She drove a dagger through it, a fancy Moorish affair, spent time and trouble elaborating it. She wouldn't be able to use it for Mothers' Day and it was too hackneyed for a Valentine.

The child's head which she started on next, was promising. She coloured the hair gold and the mouth rosebud-red, turned the eyes piously up to heaven. Stars were a possibility, they might be worked in. She did several, blazing and whirling in strong blatant colours: stars aren't meant to be stared at. The colours exhilarated her. She found how to mix up a green which actually hurt the eye.

Combinations kept occurring to her. They weren't suitable for special occasions—none, anyway, which could be marked by sending cards. But they were integrating into something which promised to be bigger.

The drawing block was filling. There were still a few spaces, and it had to be packed, like a tapestry, every inch. She did a thumbnail sketch of a bird-eating spider eating a bird. Her severed limbs were coming along nicely—branching veins, broken bones—she had been particularly clever, and saw no harm in recognising it, at illustrating the lustrous pearliness of an extruding rib. From the pierced heart she painted a spray of jewelled blood drops. To the child's head she put the finishing touches—a severed neck.

She worked throughout the night, filling every inch with pictures. Each was scrupulously, mercilessly done, and required looking into, and on being looked into, exploded like a firework in the face.

She put down her brush as the milk van came along the lane. She had drawn mayhem and made it brighter than life. She wasn't the least bit tired. On the contrary, she felt ready for anything. Please God, she said, watching the milkman tuck her pint of gold-top into the hedge, please let it be *some*thing.

Tomorrow, which was now today, he had said he would come back. Viewed from seven a.m. it was a long day, he might choose any moment of it. This time she would be ready for him.

She washed and dressed, giving thought to what she should wear. It seemed to matter and she chose a blue caftan.

She had put the picture in a prominent position, but

was in no hurry to look at it again. She sat in the window-seat. Waiting for Poe. By late afternoon she was still waiting. The thought occurred to her that tomorrow never came, and nor might he.

That mattered too. Not just because she had worked to produce something he had asked, had begged her for, but because of the nature of it. As to that, she was hopelessly confused. The picture was intended for him and was essentially his. Yet it was hers too.

What had emerged on her drawing board came from her own depths. The picture was in effect their offspring. And the effect was totally repellent. She did not want it in the house, if he did not come to fetch it away she would have to send it to him.

She picked up the telephone and dialled the Grossmiths' number.

'Agnes? Can you give me Mr Poe's address?'

'Who?'

'The young man I met at your house.'

'What young man?'

'Edgar Allan Poe.'

'Who'd have a name like that?'

'A famous writer, for one. And apparently this young man is another. I need to get in touch.'

'Why?'

'I have something to give him.' There was a pause. Elinor thought she heard Agnes licking her lips. 'Something he asked me to do for him.'

'I don't know anything about it. Sorry.' Agnes rang off.

Elinor felt as if her tiredness had been waiting on the end of the line and she had called it up. She hadn't slept for thirty-six hours, she had gone through a bad time. Bad-wicked, bad-sick, bad-beastly: she had worked through them all. For him, Edgar Allan for convenience. Poe was ridiculous, Poe was a joke at her expense. She thought of getting rid of the picture by posting it to the House of Usher.

No sooner had she thought it than a figure emerged

from the trees at the end of her garden. It was darkly dressed, wore a snap-brim trilby and moved slowly, rolling from the hips, and was tall enough to have to dip under the rose arch. He did it as a curtsey.

Elinor opened the front door, turned and went back to her studio. She stood looking at the picture.

The grainy light of dusk made it seem to move, to creep. Her precise outlines spread like florets, the whole thing blurred and swam before her eyes.

Standing behind her he smelled, improbably, of aftershave. She did hope not. Of course he had the right to go from one extreme to the other. At his age it was obligatory, something to do with time, a refusal to admit that there was any.

She was unsurprised by his clothes. His lounge suit was well cut and fitted perfectly. His tie was impeccably knotted but his shirt collar was too tight and scored a pink line round his neck.

'Well?' He took off his hat with a flourish. A strand detached from his cropped hair and fell across his forehead. He lifted it on his forefinger and tucked it into place. 'Well?'

'You look very nice.'

'I'm better, quite better.'

'I'm glad.'

'I don't anticipate any more trouble. I came to say goodbye.'

'Are you going away?'

'I'm going home.'

'Have I helped?'

'Of course.'

'How do you know!'

'You've been more than kind. I'd like something to remember you by. This, perhaps?' He picked up one of the rejected Mothers' Day roughs.

Elinor said sharply, 'You asked me to do something for you. Here it is.'

Propped on an easel it had been in his full view. She

had seen him observing his reflection in the mirror on the wall behind it.

'What is it?'

'I hoped you'd tell me.'

He reached out and repositioned the sash of her caftan. The gesture caused her heart to turn over. But all he said was, 'My poor dear,' sadly.

*

Arthur says we're getting old. He says it—we all do at any time in our lives—to excuse something he doesn't think really needs an excuse. But he means it, he's depressed, thinking about the girl on the train, he doesn't want to be old for her. It's a depressing day, the rain drips so fast out of our broken guttering it's making a froth on the flowerbed. He's waiting for me to say we're not old. Or rather, he's not. OK, I'm getting old but he's in his prime. He waits, but I don't say it. Why should I make a present of my well-seasoned husband to a girl on the train?

I ask myself what is old? Besides dysfunction and gravy stains aren't there any positive plusses to offset the minusses? I tell myself age is achieved, grown up to, waited for, like good wine. It isn't experience, which can let you down any time: or know-how, which is out of date before you know it. It's *quality*. Good or bad.

I doubt I'll have it. I'll be the same at seventy as I was at seven. Age is something I write on the dotted line.

Once I saw senior citizens assembling for the coach which would take them on an outing. They came swaying along the street, leaning on their sticks and on each other, not trusting their feet. They watched their feet. Only one man, in a yellow oilskin, held up his head. He wouldn't need the oilskin, we were into a heat-wave. When he reached the open door of the bar-parlour he paused. Another man joined him, a small man wearing a knitted cardigan. He and the cardigan had grown old together, it had a bigger paunch than his, but their tufts of hair and wool were the same sheep's colour. He reached out and took the taller man's hand.

Running down was no joke to them. Nobody would wind them up this side of Jordan. They stood looking in at the cool, dark, secret bar.

VI

THEY AREN'T KINDRED SPIRITS: Captain Galilee, a naval man, is a bit of a pirate. Roderick is a non-starter. But they complement each other, in their shrunken world mutuality is precious.

By and large they have no secrets from each other. They are past the age for secrets. If Captain Galilee hasn't told Roderick about his late wife's infidelity it's because it's too late by twenty-five years, and Roderick doesn't talk about his heart tremors because the Captain will ascribe them to Mrs Ventura.

It is no secret that Roderick is smitten with Mrs Ventura. She is the widow of a confectioner, a man who had the foresight to open a shop next to an army training centre and specialise in long-lasting peppermint lumps. He left her comfortable, as she is fond of saying. He left her as he found her, Roderick thinks wistfully. He thinks her quite unspoiled, soft, scented, pink, golden – a pillowy lady. He thinks of her without lust, simply with a view to making himself comfortable. Roderick longs to join her on her pillows. In the Captain's opinion, Mrs Ventura's comfort is all for herself.

She has favoured the Captain. He is tall and presentable, whereas her husband was little and oily, with no notion of presentation. The Captain has not responded to her advances. They were ladylike, and an insensitive man would have missed them. Captain Galilee misses nothing, but he means to run into port close-hauled.

Roderick believes himself in love. It is fifty years since he had the experience. 'I'm a bit rusty, but it's not the sort of thing you forget.'

'What do you remember?'

It is not the sort of thing he could tell anyone, except

perhaps his doctor. Mrs Ventura gives him indigestion, hot flushes, pins and needles. The thought of her hinders his bladder movements. To the best of his recollection love always did that to him.

Captain Galilee knows that Mrs Ventura is not right for his friend. She hadn't even been right for Mr Ventura, who had gone out on a wave of rancour. To do her justice, she canonised him the moment he died. She could then speak of him with the respect due to her consort, without risk of his letting her down.

The Captain became concerned about Roderick. Roderick was in an unlikely situation which might resolve itself into an altogether likely one. Although Roderick was not thinking through to the logical conclusion, there was every chance of Mrs Ventura doing so.

Roderick and Captain Galilee have been friends for years. They are in their mid-seventies, a time of life when problems and preoccupations narrow down to the same old facts of nature. They have come to rely on each other. In the matter of Mrs V, Roderick sought the Captain's help. 'I'd ask her to tea.'

'You would?'

'In the garden. If there was something to sit on.'

'There's the grass.'

'She'd want a table for the teapot. I've got a teapot. But no chairs.'

'We're sitting on chairs.'

'I can't take these outside. I need garden furniture.'

The Captain looked through the window at the grass romping over the flowerbeds. 'You need a garden.'

'Do you think she'd come?'

'It's blowing a southerly buster.'

'I don't mean today. I could borrow some wrought-iron stuff, like they have on patios.'

'Do you know anybody that has a patio?'

'Or deck chairs. But she wouldn't be able to reach the teapot from a deck chair.'

'You could reach it.'

'The lady always pours.'

'What's wrong with having tea in here?' The Captain could see what was wrong. Roderick's kitchen was like a midshipman's chest, everything on top and nothing handy. His life-style was evidenced hour by hour: his breakfast eggshells were still on the table, so was his cheese from lunch, and a piece of liver intended for his supper, a dirty shirt and a pair of long pants hung over a chair, boots muddy from last week's rain stood under the sink. 'You'd have to chamfer up.'

'I'd make some garden furniture if I could get the wood.'

'Wood's expensive.'

'It doesn't have to be new. I'd make it rustic and paint it.' Roderick's crumpled face opened up. 'It would look nice under the mulberry.' Captain Galilee smiled. The mulberry tree was coming into fruit, and last year had indelibly spotted a line of washing Roderick had hung from its branches. 'We could pick up some timber from a demolition site, or a tip—if we knew somewhere that was being demolished.'

It was the use of the plural pronoun which touched and decided Captain Galilee, the faith that he would help, that he would be with Roderick in an enterprise which he distrusted. 'I'll see what I can do.' In common with other sailors he tended to order his philosophy according to the sea, and at his time of life elected to run before the wind rather than battle with it.

He steered a course through the old Customs depot. The depot is scheduled to be pulled down to make way for a DIY megastore. Captain Galilee was annoyed to find that demolition had not started. There were piles of old tyres, black plastic bags skin-tight with things nameless, ditched supermarket trolleys and a pool of oil. No free-standing timber for the taking.

He was not disposed to go to great lengths to obtain the wood, bearing in mind what it was in aid of. Looking about him, seeing nobody, he saw a gantry rope swinging in the wind. The wind came off the North Sea, that devious, cunning, malicious ocean which would put a ship gently on a sandbar and return to break it up at leisure.

The Captain sighed. Moved by regret, he picked his way past the oily pool and entered the warehouse by a door hanging on its hinge. Inside the building it was light because most of the roof had fallen in. He disturbed pigeons roosting in the rafters and was himself disturbed by some explicit graffiti. The newspapers on the floor were also explicit, about the use they had been put to. His nostrils closed, he turned on his heel and prepared to march out. But found he was on a direct starboard beam to an assembly of oil drums. And casks. The casks were of oak staves bound with hoops, trim, snug, shipshape.

Captain Galilee, not a sentimental man, ran his thumbs over the wood. The lids were still in place, battened down, but the casks were empty, it would be possible to roll them. One would make a table and the other, properly split, two chairs. Garden-bucolic. The Captain pictured Mrs Ventura wedged into half a barrel.

He took Roderick to the warehouse to view the casks. Roderick looked doubtful. 'We don't know where they've been.'

'We'll give them a good scouring.'

Under cover of darkness they rolled the casks to Roderick's cottage. The Captain liked their feel as they bowled along. It pleased him to handle an article which was perfectly crafted for its purpose.

He was the more pleased when they prised off the lids and discovered what that purpose had been. They looked at each other. The Captain's whiskers stirred, Roderick's crumples stretched from ear to ear. They lowered their heads, hung over the casks, breathed deeply.

The fumes pierced the Captain's nose, exploded into his sinuses and dropped fire into his throat. He drew back just in time to stop the smaller, impressionable Roderick from toppling head first into the cask.

Roderick coughed, blinked, openly wept. 'I can't have her sitting in something that smells of whisky!'

The Captain, who thought it would be a most delightful situation, put the lids back, ramming them home with his fist. 'She'll never know.'

'We'll never get rid of the smell!'

'We'll soak them, soak the spirit out of the wood.'

The Captain went into the kitchen to fill the old stone copper.

'Seems a pity,' said Roderick.

'What does?'

'Soaking the spirit out.' The Captain thought the same. Shut up in its casks the spirit was reinforcing itself on the compound interest principle. Roderick, who could be childish, asked 'Where will it go?'

'Heaven,' the Captain said shortly.

They filled each cask with boiling water. The steam rose in slender stems which broke out like flags from a mast. The Captain said they must leave the water to do its work. So they went to the Dream of Fair Women which, as the Captain remarked, was appropriate in the circumstances.

After a couple of pints they had to admit that the beer at The Dream was not up to standard. They moved to The Plough, where Roderick bought the Captain a piece of bacon pie in recognition of his part in finding the casks.

'Shall we paint them green?'

The Captain bit on a pickled onion and tears came to his eyes. 'Do what you like with the gingerbread work, I'll do the rest.'

'Won't they fall to bits when you start sawing?'

'Oak doesn't fall to bits. I doubt there'll be a thimbleful of sawdust.'

They left The Plough before closing-time and went back to the cottage. Roderick worried. 'Hadn't we better empty them? I can't paint the wood till it's dry.'

'I can't cut it till it's dry.'

There was no steam rising from the casks. There they

were in Roderick's kitchen, trim, tight vessels honourably scarred with use and wear, strong and sturdy as the day the cooper made them—for just the one sweet purpose. Captain Galilee observed that pickled onions left him with a lump in his throat.

Roderick, putting his hands on one of the casks, was rewarded by a gentle blood-warmth in the wood. Looking in, he saw a glint, heard a faint but steady hiss. The Captain thought there was a movement. He dipped in his finger, smelt, licked it. 'God!' He spoke with reverence.

'What's up?'

'The spirit.'

'What?'

'Is risen.' The Captain fetched a cup, plunged it into the cask and brought it up full of murky yellowish liquid. There was unmistakable activity on the surface, the murk was shot through with a discharge of tiny bubbles.

Roderick, being nearsighted, followed the bubbles to their point of explosion at the rim of the cup. 'What is it?'

The Captain put the cup to his nose. He took a mouthful and could be seen rolling it over his tongue. Without hesitation he swallowed.

'Are you crazy?' said Roderick. 'Drinking dirty water—'

'This is bull. Spirit from the wood, released in the water.' The Captain held out the cup.

'Not for me, thanks.'

'You'll never get another taste like this. It's been years in the wood. It's history.' Roderick took the cup, smelt it, moistened his lips. 'Take a swig, man, don't sip like a hen!'

The Captain could still command obedience, and Roderick obeyed. He drank, spluttered and coughed as the stuff reached his gullet.

'It's raw, it will improve. I suggest we leave it until it stops working.'

'What about my furniture?'

'All in good time.'

The Captain put the lids back and they pushed the casks under the kitchen table. The Captain said they shouldn't risk some busybody of a chance caller discovering what they were doing.

'Is it illegal?'

'Of course not. It's salvage. We're morally entitled to it, in fact we're responsible for it.' The Captain, who had been empowered to conduct religious services at sea, gave it the full pulpit tone. 'Would your conscience rest easy if we allowed this spirit to waste away?'

They waited a week. It was a trying time, Roderick pining for Mrs Ventura, Captain Galilee hovering round the casks like a bee. Flesh and blood being what it was, visions of Mrs Ventura triumphed over Roderick's finer feelings. He looked at the casks and wondered just what it was they were waiting for.

The Captain was treating it as an inexact science. The interaction of the spirit and water he declared directly deducible, but did not weary Roderick with a deduction. The uncertain factor was time. Nobody could say how long the process would take: a week, a month—

'A month!'

'We'll take a sounding on Saturday.'

They met as usual in The Plough. As they sat over their pints of bitter someone asked, and paid for, a large Scotch.

'Did you hear what that cost?' said the Captain. 'There's gold brewing under your kitchen table.'

'I can't wait for ever.'

'It's a process of transmutation, can't be hurried.'

By tacit consent they drank up and went to the cottage. They brought out the casks from under the table. The Captain warned that different combinations operating differently would produce different results in each.

'Combinations?'

'Atmospheric.' The Captain polished a glass on his sleeve.

'Will it poison us?'

'Let me be the judge.'

When the first cask was opened they bent over, looking in. They saw a bright surface, amber coloured and clear for several inches. Beyond that it plunged into darkness in the belly of the cask. Roderick thought it winked at him.

The Captain said something which might have been a prayer or an imprecation. He filled his glass and sipped from it. Frowning, he drank, paused, then finished the draught. He seemed to grow taller. His eyes brimmed. There was little room between his whiskers for the expression of emotion, but it was undoubtedly joy showing in his cheeks. They glowed, tender as a girl's, and surprised Roderick who was accustomed to hear him claim that every drop of his blood was Stockholm tar.

He refilled the glass and handed it over. Roderick sniffed it nervously, took a mouthful. For a moment he was aware only of a vulgar taste. His tongue arched in self-defence. Then pure fire shot down his throat, spread over his chest, reached his heart. He saw Mrs Ventura sitting in glory.

'In my opinion,' said the Captain, whom Roderick could not quite see, 'this combination has already attained a proof of fifty per cent alcohol. Let's try the other one.'

When Roderick was aroused by the Captain it was lunchtime to the best of his belief and memory. He seemed to be lying on the floor. An extraordinary amount of light was concentrated in his head. It was not unpleasant, he believed he could illuminate the dark corners of his larder just by looking in. He thought the Captain, too, could do with illumination, he was quite dusky. Roderick beamed on him. 'How about some lunch?'

'Do you know what time it is? Seven o'clock.'

'I'm hungry.'

'In the evening.'

Roderick hadn't wanted to lose time. His was limited, and he lived each moment: some moments he lived longer than others, some he re-lived because they weren't long

enough or didn't come. Like those with Mrs Ventura.'
'What happened?'

'As I was saying, we have achieved a high percentage of alcohol. We have here a liquor powered by years of matured spirit, a tipple that beats the baby's wee they sell at The Plough. And every drop comes to us free.'

'It can't be!'

'Who do you propose we should offer to pay for it? Customs and Excise? The DIY company that owns the site of the old warehouse?'

'Seven o'clock – it can't be evening.'

The Captain stalked to and fro, whiskers bristling. 'How should we value it? What price can we put on the water of life?'

'I'm going to fry up.'

'It will improve. It will age. Mature. What's more, we can do it again. Get every last drop out of the wood.'

'What about my chairs? My table for the garden?' Captain Galilee rose to his full height, six foot three in his socks, and Roderick, who scarcely reached his shoulder, shrank several inches, but cried from the Captain's underarm, 'For when Mrs Ventura comes!'

'You heard about the changing of the water into wine?'

'That was in the Bible—'

'I speak no blasphemy. We have assisted at a greater miracle. We have created whisky out of souse-water.'

'We could bottle it and I could have the casks.'

'If you cage an eagle it ceases to be an eagle. The spirit is in the wood.'

'Where can I put Mrs Ventura?'

The Captain was tempted to tell him. 'My dear fellow—'

'If I don't ask her, someone else will. Someone with a patio and garden chairs.'

'What about the parlour?'

'I never use the parlour.'

'It's the right place for a lady.' When the Captain smiled it was as if a way opened through the trees. 'For a queen.'

'It's in a state—'

'Ask her. I'll help you tidy, we'll get it shipshape.'
'You haven't seen what it's like.'
'Nothing a cleaning trick or two won't put right.'
'I can't get the door open, it's stuck.'
'Roger,' said the Captain cheerfully. He crossed the passage in two strides and put his shoulder to the door. It gave with an almighty crack, causing Roderick concern for his own skull which was still full of unnatural radiance, illumining countless veins behind his eyeballs. The parlour, however, remained dark.

'Like the Indies,' said the Captain. A chinaberry bush grew across the window. Roderick trod on something soft, part of last Autumn's apple crop, stored here and forgotten. 'Mice,' said the Captain. 'Little beggars have left you the cores.'

'What can I get for her tea?'
'She'll have a sweet tooth.'

Roderick thought he would give her strawberries and watch her sweet tooth bite into the soft fruit. It made him dizzy.

'I like the wallpaper,' said the Captain. 'The floral pattern's very suitable. We'll hang pictures over the damp patches.'

'There's a fireplace. I could make toast.' Roderick was thinking of the butter shining on her lips.

'What's this?'

'Every year magpies try to build in the chimney and the nests fall through on the hearth. They never learn.'

The Captain filled and lit his pipe. The lighted match he threw into the twigs. They caught at once, tongues of flame licked up the chimney.

Roderick started worrying about where and when he should approach Mrs Ventura. His opportunities were limited. If he waited around in Sainsbury's he would eventually encounter her. But he should take care not to invite her to tea while they were stood next to the pigs' kidneys and sheeps' hearts. She inspired him to such considerations, refined and tender. He decided that the proper place would be in the biscuit section.

Something was happening. Clouds of soot were billowing down the chimney. Pipe in mouth, the Captain stood to attention as soft black dust settled on his head and shoulders.

It took a lot of energy getting the parlour ready. When the Captain had chopped down the chinaberry and let in the daylight it was obvious that a lick and a promise wasn't going to be enough. Roderick simply couldn't see Mrs Ventura in his parlour. Carried away by despair he cried that it would be like putting a rose on a dunghill.

The Captain said, 'The smell of rotten apples is not unpleasant. It's good for Channel sickness.'

Some of the cores had fallen under the floorboards, they could be sensed but not reached. The Captain lent Roderick a rug to cover them. They cleaned the window and dusted the furniture. They found a mouse's nest with six frail little skeletons in it. The Captain was charmed and put it on the mantelpiece to charm Mrs Ventura.

The only picture Roderick possessed was a print of the execution of Lady Jane Grey. He felt it was unsuited to the occasion. But there were many peeling areas which needed concealment.

They went to the bus station after the last bus had gone and prised several excursion posters from the walls. These gave the parlour a holiday look, the Captain feared that incitements to take a day trip to Bridlington might give Mrs Ventura ideas for the future.

He was with Roderick when they encountered her. Roderick panicked and tried to run. The Captain held him, pushed him forward to face her. Roderick's finer feelings deserted him. He blurted, 'Will you come to tea?' forgetting to say "please". Confronted with her mauve eyelids and lilac curls, he forgot everything except his need.

Confronted by Roderick's antique pullover and wild eye, she drew back. 'Tea? With you?'

'Thursday, four o'clock. Pobbs' Cottage, Gun Hill—it's not Pobbs's, it's mine—'

'I'm sorry, I shall be otherwise engaged.'

The Captain stepped forward. 'We have prepared a room for you, ma'am.'

'A room?'

'The parlour is at your disposal.'

Mrs Ventura looked up at him. She was herself petite and had a distance to cover. Her lashes fluttered under the strain. 'Shall you be there?'

'We have tried to make it worthy of you.'

'Perhaps I might rearrange my engagements.'

The Captain told Roderick she was sure to come.

'How do you know?'

The Captain brushed up his moustache. 'My dear fellow, I didn't come up in the last bucket.'

By midday Thursday Roderick was in a state of high tension. The table had been set in the parlour, he had made sandwiches and the Captain had brought a golden-syrup cake from Tesco's. 'Is there no jam?'

'These are fish-paste sandwiches.'

'Ah well, you never can tell with women.'

'Suppose she gets a cracked cup?'

'She won't notice when the tea's in.'

The Captain had had his own table on board ship: he added a finishing touch with marigolds picked from the garden.

'What shall I say to her?'

'She'll cluck like an ash-hoist, you won't need to say anything. Now you're all set I'll be off.'

'You can't go!'

'Why not?'

'Don't leave me—I feel terrible!'

Even with his past experience, the Captain marvelled at the power of women over men: it was ephemeral, but dire. Here was Roderick trembling like a leaf, one last brown leathery leaf about to drop off the tree.

'My heart's stopping—I'm going to have a stroke—'

'Nonsense.'

'A diabellic stroke, I can feel myself going!'

'Pull yourself together. She'll be here any moment.' The Captain pushed him into a chair. 'I'll get you something to strengthen your nerve.' He filled a glass from one of the casks.

'Not that—'

'It will put heart into you. Drink, or drown.'

Roderick, going down for the second time, came up, accepted the glass and drank from it. As was to be expected, the effect was miraculous. The Captain had expected no less. Roderick ceased to shake, his eyes focused, his knees came together.

The Captain knew that Mrs Ventura would present numberless hazards. Women's wiles were given them to make up for their general under-endowment. But as usual, Nature had gone too far and over-compensated. The Captain doubted if Roderick, at his endangered time of life, could stand up to the pressure. He would need all the help he could get. Providentially, that help was at hand.

'One more shot and you'll be ready for anything.'

As Roderick was draining the second glass, Mrs Ventura appeared at the garden gate. 'Bring her in gently,' said the Captain and went to put the kettle on.

While he brewed up, he had opportunity to reflect on the relationship between Mrs Ventura and the potion in the casks. One would not have emerged without the other, and the one was required to resolve a situation brought about by the other. He was aware as soon as she set foot in the cottage. Her persona preceded her—a chemically invasive scent which alerted and offended several of his senses. He took a draught to stabilise them.

He valued Roderick's friendship with the highest value he put on anything nowadays. Over the years they had assessed each other's plusses and minusses and settled for the difference. It was too late for him to form another such friendship. But he was not one to lament the past or try to hold up the present. Roderick aspired to the Widow

Ventura, a mistake in the Captain's opinion. He had once made such a one himself. In choosing a woman, each man had to chart his own passage round the rocks.

Roderick, appearing at the door of the kitchen, looked calm and collected, porting well. Perhaps a little too well. The Captain raised his brows in an unspoken question. To which Roderick replied with a would-be aye-aye gesture, but his two fingers missed their aim and ended in his ear.

'Steady,' said the Captain.

Mrs Ventura materialised at Roderick's elbow, then seemed to de-materialise and re-materialise in front of him. She moved like a cloud, a pink and gold sunset puff. The Captain considered her dress immodest. It was of some flimsy stuff, cut low to present her bosoms and short to show her legs: solid flesh, all of them—the cloud effect was illusory.

'So here you are.' She stood looking round the kitchen.

'Good afternoon, ma'am.' The Captain couldn't stop himself warming to her and was vexed and at the same time pleased to find he still had that warmth in him.

'I should like to wash my hands before tea. I seem to have touched something.' She flicked her fingers. The Captain obligingly turned on the tap over the sink. 'Kindly show me the bathroom.'

'There isn't one.'

'No bathroom? Doesn't he wash?'

'Certainly he does. '

Roderick, frowning, tried to repeat the assurance but was blocked by the first syllable. He could only utter a hiss like a punctured tyre.

'I'm afraid I can't stay long.' Mrs Ventura looked meaningly at the Captain.

He did not allow himself to speculate on what the meaning might be. 'Brewing up,' he said, deliberately lower-deck. 'Take your place at table, ma'am and you'll be served.'

'My name is Eunice.'

'Tea,' Roderick said weightily. He was doing his best. The Captain hoped he was not overstretched.

'My late husband called me Rosamund. He was of a romantic disposition.'

Roderick giggled from sheer happiness. But it was the wrong moment to show it and he got an unqualified glare from the lady.

'Myself, I'm a practical man,' said the Captain. 'My friend here has the soft heart.'

'Names are important. May I ask what yours is?'

'Galilee, Captain Merchant Navy, retired. At your service.'

'I meant your baptismal name.'

'I was never baptised. My parents were unbelievers.'

Roderick sang softly—'Rosie, Rosie, Rosie Lee'—in a world of his own. The Captain would gladly have joined him, but there was Mrs Ventura and the teapot to cope with. 'I hope you like a strong brew, ma'am.'

'Call me Rosamund.'

The small hairs stirred along the Captain's backbone. He felt himself getting out of depth in her eye shadow. Being a practical man he would no doubt have survived, but he knew that the means of survival would cause him regret, and quite possibly shame.

Roderick rescued him from both. Blissfully smiling, he turned up the whites of his eyes, gave at the knees and lay down on the floor coiled like a rope. Mrs Ventura screamed.

'Calm yourself,' said the Captain.

'What's happened? Is he ill?'

'Just leave him be.'

'He's fainted!'

'Over-excitement. Seeing you has been too much for him.'

'Is he dead?'

The Captain smiled. 'Not so much as that, I fancy.'

'I can't see him breathing.' She stooped over Roderick's recumbent form. 'I smell whisky!'

'Allow me.' The Captain attempted to bring her upright. Too late, she had seen the casks under the table.

'Barrels of it!'

'Now be reasonable, ma'am. Where would a poor pensioner find money to buy whisky in that quantity?'

Her golden eye was as round as a pigeon's. 'If he didn't buy it, he made it.' Not for the first time the Captain noted the process whereby a woman made up her mind. Having jumped to a conclusion, she now settled on it. 'He's running an illicit still—he's a bootlegger!' She cried, 'I shall be duty bound to report him to the authorities!'

'I should be sorry to see you look foolish.'

'These barrels—'

'Contain water, ma'am. What else? I'm not denying there may have been whisky in them once. But a barrel is all the poor fellow has to soak himself in. Would you report him for drinking his bath water?'

*

Who was it called a son 'that unfeathered, two-legged thing'? Maurice is sixteen and thoroughly self-sufficient. If only he would let go sometimes. It must be a strain, keeping a stiff upper lip. I worry that he will end with a stiff neck and no resources.

He joined the army when he was twelve. It was against my wish and I went to his school to complain to the headmaster.

'Mrs Appleton,' he said, 'your husband has given his permission, but of course we prefer to have the approval of both parents.'

'I don't want my son playing war-games.'

'I fear the media is to blame for such misnomers. Our Cadet Corps is not a game for children but a vital discipline to develop the minds and bodies of young men.'

'The Young Person's Guide to Mass Murder.'

Maurice's headmaster has a special smile for women. It is accommodating, he accommodates his intellect to theirs.

His method of dealing with female parents is as a decimal place several times removed from the father unit.

'We all want peace, therefore we must be ready to defend it,' he said kindly. 'Your son could be officer material, Mrs Appleton. He is keen and very competent. I can understand that you have reservations. You are concerned for his welfare and his safety. I shall try to reassure you on both counts.'

'I hate the idea.'

'Of course I respect your convictions. But you do realise that membership of the school corps does not commit Maurice to an army career? It is an extra-curricular activity. To deny his participation would be to exclude him from part of the life of the school. The majority of his classmates have enlisted and he would find himself debarred from a significant area of their interests and—I may say it—enjoyment. Boys need adventure, if they don't get it one way they will get it another.' He vouchsafed me a sober twinkle. 'Their need must be directed into legitimate and healthy channels. Army training is a training for life. It teaches self-reliance and self-discipline.'

'Maurice is too uptight as it is.'

'Why do you think that?'

Of course I couldn't tell him. He waited, politely, doodling on his notepad a series of unwinding spirals.

'I think militarism will lock him up,' I said.

He gave me his accommodating smile. 'Maurice is a fine boy.'

It would have been tactful of him not to mention my visit to Maurice. If, to his way of thinking, tact was lost on me, what of common consideration? Surely he knew enough, if not about Maurice in particular, about boys in general, to realise he was making trouble between us.

Maurice came to me in what could be described as a towering rage. At twelve years old he was already as tall as I was and so puffed up that he did tower over me.

'Why the hell did you go to Rycroft?'

'I'm sorry—I felt I must.'

'How do you think it looks for someone my age having his mother whingeing about getting his feet wet and messing up his clothes?'

'I didn't whinge.'

'Good God, woman, I'm not your baby boy!'

I ought to have smacked him. If I had, he would have hit me back. 'You never were,' I said and thought, too late, that he would remember and be hurt by that when he cooled down. 'I had a brief unsatisfactory exchange with your headmaster—'

'And your exchange puts paid to my prospects of promotion!'

'That's absurd.'

'Is it? Can I command respect with that background? Discipline people under me? Get their trust?'

'Maurice, I didn't talk about wet feet, if your headmaster says I did, he's lying.'

'I'll tell you what he said. He said "Your mother is concerned about you, Appleton. She fears the rough and tumble of army life will make you insensitive and spoil your clothes. Try to reassure her." '

'That's absolute misrepresentation. I went to discuss principles—'

'Principles!'

'I have some. I think it's wrong for children to be inducted into war-play—'

It was the worst thing I could have said. He practically spat at me and flung out of the room.

VII

A WOMAN I CALL Lalla Puritz had the misfortune to fall in love with her son's form master. It was a misfortune for two reasons. The first was that the man died, and what made her grief insupportable was that he had been dead for a whole weekend without her being aware of it, and while she was dreaming about being in his arms. The second reason, when she came to know of it, quite changed the character of her grief.

Simon Reckitt had called to talk to her about Kevin's reports which featured words like 'disappointing', 'underachievement' and 'bone-idle'.

Reckitt made it clear that these were his colleagues' opinions, not his. Kevin, he said, gazing at Lalla with a warmth which flustered her, was a fine boy, singularly fine. (This, of course, was Lalla's own opinion.)

Between themselves, Reckitt said, he had doubts about forcing a boy of such promise into the general framework. But it was the policy of the school, the curriculum demanded, the headmaster set certain standards, etc., etc.

He himself had every confidence in Kevin, and now that he had seen Kevin's home—he looked lingeringly about him, and last and longest at her—but results were required and he hoped she understood his difficulty.

Lalla did. And sympathised. She said, 'I have tried to talk to him.'

'Oh, so have I. It's no chore to talk to Kevin, it's simply unproductive. My experience is that there are boys who can't be moulded and one shouldn't try.'

Lalla asked would he like a cup of tea. He said, quite miserably, 'You mustn't worry.'

Lalla said she didn't. She did, of course, she worried

that the world wouldn't pay Kevin what he believed was owing to him.

'I don't disagree with Headmaster. Absolutely not. Were I in his shoes—mind you, I'm never likely to be, I'm not cut out for an academic.'

Lalla thought he would make an army officer. He had a big compact frame and reined-in energy, she could see him in khaki.

'About his reports, I mean. Kevin is fully fashioned, basically OK. Good lord, he's more than that!' It came bursting out of his chest with a laugh and a groan.

'I don't see what I can do.' The thought did cross her mind that she was paying Reckitt to do what should be done.

He seemed to agree, for he grasped her hand. 'You've done enough.'

She was to remember that. She put the obvious interpretation on it at the time, afterwards she saw that there was another. The words returned to mock her. She suspected there had been reproach in them. His touch, too, she had to re-examine. She had taken it for the spontaneous expression of desire. Was it in fact a reaching out for a helping hand? Or a slap on the wrist?

She made the next move. Quite properly, for she had been approached on a practical matter. True, a few impracticalities had emerged, as they did from any encounter. The thickness of his eyelashes, for instance, had surprised her, but it was not to check on them that she decided to go to the school, it was because of his concern on Kevin's behalf. She went in all practicality to the next parents' evening.

Reckitt was noticeable, she noticed him as soon as she entered the hall, and he looked at her across the crowded room with ardour. It was a long time since she had had a private exchange with a man, the last occasion had given rise to Kevin who was now fourteen years old. As an unwanted woman she tried not to want.

Reckitt was in conversation with a group of husbands

and wives. The women wore hats, which put Lalla in her place. She had the sort of hair which couldn't be contained, a mass of minuscule wiry ringlets. Her mother-in-law had sworn that this proved that Lalla had negro blood.

She turned her back on the group. Reckitt was using his hands a lot. Suddenly censorious, she thought he was *making* himself noticeable. And why wear pre-shrunk jeans, a man of his age? She thought, I'm using my antibodies in self-defence, as I would against a common cold. It amused her.

A man with a black gown hanging from his shoulders appeared at her side. 'We don't see you here very often.'

'No.'

'Forgive me, I'm sure we've met.'

'We haven't.'

'I'm Andrew Caley, headmaster.'

'My son came to the school before you did. It was your predecessor I met.'

'That would be Dr Astley. I was appointed to the headship a year ago.'

'I'm Lalla Puritz.'

'Ah. Kevin. A senior of Five B. Due for transfer to Five A.'

'Is that good?'

The headmaster smiled. 'It is time.'

'Are you saying he's a dunce?'

'Not in the generally accepted sense. The word derives from Duns Scotus, an opposer of classical studies. Kevin opposes all study, on the grounds that it is of no use to him.'

'You must show him he's wrong.'

The headmaster's smile locked at the corners. 'I intend to, Mrs Puritz.'

At that moment he was called away and Lalla was left smarting.

'It never strikes him that Kevin could be right.' Reckitt had abandoned the ladies with hats. As he stood looking down at her, her smart warmed to a glow.

'How can he be right?'

'Kevin will do very well as he is.'

'I want him to have an education, it's what I'm paying for.'

'You and his father.' It was a statement, but she did not miss the question.

'His father is not concerned. We parted years ago.'

'I wondered. Kevin is uncommunicative on the subject.'

'He never knew his father.'

'So he has only you.'

'You don't think it's enough?'

His lashes were as thick as she remembered. He used them to express both shyness and daring. 'I think he's very lucky.'

It wasn't her fault that they never achieved a full physical relationship. She longed for it, and to all intents and purposes so did he. She believed that only his honesty prevented the consummation of their love and that he would have to be won round. She believed she was winning when he died.

The first time they kissed she was surprised and a little frightened to realise how a strong man vibrated, from the soles of his feet to his olfactory nerves. His nostrils were opened wide and pinched shut with a definite rhythm. He was like an engine ticking over and ready to burst into life. She had the feeling that they were at the start of something which couldn't be reversed. She did not want it reversed.

Holding her in his arms, he told her of the barrier between them. He had a wife, a chronic invalid who doted on him, a poor tormented creature who hungered for his caresses. He inferred that she made ignoble demands on him, and being her husband, and pitiful, he was obliged to meet them.

Lalla, her own passion aroused, clung to him and vibrated with him.

'I'm afraid I may now be incapable of a normal reaction.' His lashes, trembling on his cheek, enchanted her. 'You do see what I mean? My difficulty?'

'It will be all right, it will be perfect!'

'Time,' he said, while she kissed his eyelids. 'It will take me time to adjust.'

'Let me help you.'

He pressed his lips on hers and she ardently responded. They clung together, as desperate as if they had met in mid-ocean on one lifebelt. He begged, 'Be patient.'

When he sent her poetry she wasn't altogether pleased, she wanted deeds, not words. Kevin handed her a foolscap envelope. 'From Simple Simon.'

'Who?'

'Simple Simon Reckitt.'

The envelope was unaddressed. She thought he's written to say it can't go on. 'Why do you call him that?'

'Doesn't it strike you?'

'Why should it?'

Kevin pulled an expressive face, she dared not think what it was meant to express. She and Reckitt had been circumspect, he came to her only in his free periods when Kevin was in school.

'Open it.'

She was obliged to, while Kevin watched. Inside was a single sheet of paper with a block of handwriting in the centre. It was headed 'Elegy to an Untasted Love'. She scanned it with alarm and dismay.

'This is for me?'

'Who else?'

Kevin hung his bag over his shoulder and went upstairs whistling.

The verses were strong on feeling, and on rhyme— 'e'en' and 'been', 'heart' and 'dart', 'lost' and 'toss't', 'moan' and 'lone'. Kevin had certainly read them, the envelope had been re-sealed. The last lines read: 'Shall I compare thee to the dewy morn? Thou art more lovely than the summer corn. I long to hold thee to my breast, in that embrace which knows no rest'.

She took the verses to bed with her. It didn't matter if Kevin had read them, he wouldn't understand. 'That embrace which knows no rest . . .' She cried into her pillow, 'What are we waiting for!'

When he came the next day he apologised for wearing his track suit. He had been jogging and was on his way back to school. He couldn't stay, he had a class to take.

She flung herself into his arms. 'I loved every word!'

He held her tightly. Sometimes she thought that if he didn't hold her so tight she could get closer to him. 'What word?'

'The poem, your poem. It says everything I want to say to you and don't know how.' He blushed as a strong man blushes, deep crimson with a touch of purple. 'It's beautiful. No one has ever written me poetry before. But my darling, sending it through Kevin was risky. He's nosy, like all young people. I think he may have opened the envelope. Why didn't you post it?'

He sighed, his chest swelled unbearably against her own. 'British Telecom is so mundane.'

'Surely—when we both want "the embrace that knows no rest"—' Surely we are starting it, she thought, his arms were like iron about her. 'My dearest one—'

He released her and stood plucking at his track suit with a gesture which cut her to the heart. She held out her arms: she was sure, not shameless, she was sure of herself and what she could do for him.

'Just a little longer,' he said, 'and then we shall have all the time in the world.'

'Shall we?'

'I can't just leave my wife.'

'I'm not asking you to leave her.'

'She depends on me, she has no one else.'

'I have no one else.'

'You have Kevin,' he said sadly.

She watched him jogging away from her along the street, elbows at his sides, knees lifting like pistons. Then she went and scrubbed the floor and wept into the pail.

Next day Kevin came in from school as she was preparing their supper. 'Bacon and sausage pie? What's after?'

'Tapioca.'

He pulled a face but his heart wasn't in it. 'Something awful happened.'

She was making a rosette for the top of the pie. It wouldn't look much like a rosette when it came out of the oven, but she always made one with the leftover pastry. 'You've got another bad report?'

'For God's sake, there are other things besides reports.'

'Don't be rude.'

'It's Simple Simon. He's gone and died.' She was to remember the feel of the pastry as she crushed it into a ball. She was never to make another rosette for the top of a pie. 'He fell and cracked his skull—seems it wasn't so thick after all.'

'When?' As if the timing mattered—

'Yesterday.'

Perhaps it did. 'Not yesterday, it couldn't have been—he was here yesterday—'

'He was out jogging and slipped on something nasty.' Kevin's grin was without humour. 'He struck his head on the kerb and died before they got him to hospital.'

Worst of all was the brevity of their affair, it hadn't really been an affair, only the promise of one. Promise was all she was short of, and in a state of physical deprivation, like facing the prospect of being forever hungry, she tried fulfilling it. By the day of the funeral she was mourning a grand passion bigger than both of them, purer than sex and holier than matrimony. She held it until such moments as when she was making the same old beds and soaping the same old armpits. She broke down then, and cried because her body and the bedclothes existed and he didn't. With every passing day he was becoming less real.

He had never talked much about himself, what little she knew she had been obliged to put together. Which she had done to her own satisfaction, picturing a cheerless home, a predatory woman reaching for him from among unwashed dishes and medicine bottles. 'I am not a free man,' he had said.

She did not go to the funeral. The headmaster went, and two boys from Reckitt's form were deputed to attend. Kevin was not one of them. 'I wouldn't have gone', he said. She dared not ask why.

One of the things Reckitt had not told her was where he lived. Fortunately there were only a few Reckitts in the local telephone directory, and only one with the initial 'S'.

She thought a lot about it before she went. At times the grand passion deserted her and she was left with a plain old rage of wanting. It happened at squalid moments and she thought it would make a sort of logic to confront them with the squalid moments from his life. She needed to know what they had been, she needed details of his living. Facts couldn't bring him back, but they would confirm that he had lived.

He had lived in a flat in a tower block overlooking the Park. It was not what she had expected. She entered a reception area carpeted with heavy-duty pile. There was a lift and a Yucca plant chained to the wall. She rang for the lift.

On the eighth floor, outside a door with a spy-hole, she began to fear that he had deceived her. True, her expectations were her own, but they had come from her impression of him. The impression was all she had. Panicking, she pressed the bell.

A man opened the door. He said 'Are you Help the Aged?'

'I beg your pardon?'

'You're Mrs Timms, of course. It's all ready for you.'

Lalla said with relief, 'I think I've come to the wrong place. I'm looking for Mrs Reckitt.'

'Mr,' he said cheerfully. 'I've done it up for you. Shirts, trousers, pants, socks. Size nine shoes.' He held the door wide. 'Do come in.' She obeyed. He went into a room off the passage. 'Here we are. None of it's pristine, he was hard on his clothes. But I daresay you'll get a few quid for it.'

The room was a bedroom, bright, warm, tweedy, with built-in wardrobe and dressing-table complex, books and bonsai, anglepoise lamp, desk, television. The view from the window was of trundling cloud. On the double bed were bundles of clothes tied with string, carrier bags of shoes, a corduroy cap, a straw hat trimmed with flowers.

'Most of his things are too big for me,' said the man. 'But I'm keeping his track suit, there'll be room to sweat.'

She saw it lying across a chair and remembered him turning away from her, plucking the suit from his chest, angry and helpless.

'He had a lot of videos but they're blue, you won't want those. I'll help you carry this stuff out to your car. Or did you bring a van?'

'No—' She leaned against the doorpost.

'Are you all right?'

'I'm not—'

He said sharply, 'Not from the charity shop?'

'No. I came—I'm a friend of Simon's.'

He cleared a space on the bed. 'You'd better sit down.'

'Is this his room?'

'It was.'

He flopped down on the bed. He was snorting with laughter. She said incredulously, 'Who are you?'

'I don't know.' She saw that he wasn't laughing, he was crying.

'Where is his wife?'

'I was his wife.' He fished under the bed, brought out a half empty bottle of gin. 'Join me?'

'He said his wife was an invalid—'

'I expect to be. I expect to be a chronic invalid.' He took a swig from the bottle.

'I don't understand.'

'We were gay, dear lady, gay as larks up here in our singing cage.'

125

'Are you saying—'

He squinted into the depths of the bottle. 'We were lovers and sweethearts, yes.'

'You're trying to besmirch his memory!'

'Ho, ho, ho!' He punched the bundles of clothes. 'Besmirch, is it?'

'Listen to me—'

'You listen to me. We were happy together, we lived in wedded bliss until he got fixated on someone else.'

'Yes—'

'It was a boy in his form at school. But the kid wasn't having any. Simon couldn't get to him.'

'No—'

'If he had, it would soon have been over and done with. He was like that. But the boy held him off, kept him dangling and it took him right out of himself. He was desperate.'

'That's nonsense!'

'He wrote poetry to the boy, he was a rotten poet. No wonder the kid laughed at him.'

'You're quite wrong—'

'If there's one thing I know about it's poetry. I took my degree in English lit.'

'I'm talking about—'

'I'm talking, you're listening. He was crazy about that kid, he couldn't get near him—hell, he couldn't get anywhere. He wanted to see what his home was like, who his parents were, whether he had crunchies or sugar-puffs for breakfast. That sort of thing. He wanted every single detail. So he went and chatted up the boy's mother.' Lalla's mouth opened. Her tongue was dry, she couldn't speak. 'She fell for him. Lady, she fell like Niagara. It broke his nerve. He used to come home shaking all over and tell me about it. What she'd said, what he'd had to do.' The gin bottle, upended, showed daylight. 'He wasn't ambisextrous, he was only trying to get to the boy.' He threw the bottle aside, took up a bundle of shirts and buried his face in them.

There was a ring at the doorbell.

'That'll be the people for the clothes,' said Lalla.

She went home and took the poem from under her pillow and read it through. It was something she had to do. The line about the embrace that knew no rest meant what she had taken it to mean, but of course it wasn't hers to take.

When Kevin came in from school she handed him the poem. 'This is yours.'

He glanced at it. 'Mine?'

'Who else's?'

'What shall I do with it?'

'You could send it to the school magazine.'

*

Maurice was still in junior school when he came and told me they'd had a sex education class. He said, 'I don't think I'll have sex, it seems like a dirty habit.' He wasn't entirely artless as a child. He knew half of what he was saying, and meant it at the time. I think the quality of the dirt inhibits him still. Mud and blood are honourable, the other is smut and only good for a giggle. He'll think better of that one day.

VIII

'IT'S A WASTE,' said Kevin.

'It's only for an hour.'

'A waste of this.' Kevin waved at the afternoon. Meryl said, 'I know.' She always knew and Kevin, who would have said he didn't want anyone reading his thoughts, felt like a king when kings had clout.

'I want to be in our secret place,' she said, 'where no one else has ever been.'

He didn't point out that it was only a clearing in the bushes with Coke cans in the grass. He was trying to be thoughtful but he couldn't follow her thoughts the way she could follow his. He grumbled. 'It's three weeks to Christmas and look at the gnats. Next Sunday it'll be raining. I could come then to see your parents.'

'They're expecting us. They want to see you, see who I'm going with.'

'You didn't tell them we're—you know.'

'Of course not. They wouldn't understand. In their day it was a crime to have sex before marriage.'

'My mother's not bothered.'

'It's different for you. I've got more to lose.' It was the said thing, but she knew he wished she hadn't said it. She stood on tiptoe to kiss his cheek. 'And so much to gain.'

They had discussed the question of sex and decided to have it. She was of the opinion that it was a question: were they ready for the greatest experience of their lives? Kevin, who had been thinking of it as a simple matter of getting his oats, tried to be objective and had taken himself through the mechanics stage by stage. He had come up against his own unknowing.

'It will be so much easier when they've seen you.'

'Easier for what?'

'For me to go on seeing you.' Kevin had not been aware of any restriction in that quarter. But seeing her now, with the sun on her hair and the delicate shadow on her eyelids, he was struck with the thought that she should be protected. 'My parents adore each other. They can't bear to be parted.' She sighed. 'I'm so lucky.'

Kevin interpreted the sigh as being on his account. Such tenderness shamed him, he had thought himself lucky to have only one parent to contend with. He said, 'I can't stay long, I've got to go to Tufnell Park.'

'Why?'

Wild horses wouldn't have dragged him from her side on a Sunday afternoon, but the prospect of tea with her parents was splitting them asunder. 'I have to visit this old guy in a wheelchair. He gets lonely.' She gazed at him with gladness and sadness in her eyes and he thought with her to believe in him he could become a much better person. 'It's something I feel I have to do.'

She cried, 'I do want them to know you!'

He worried that what she wanted them to know wasn't there yet. It might be, some day, and he would have preferred to wait for it before facing her parents. But that same afternoon she took him to her house and shut the door on the golden sun and the dizzy gnats.

He found himself in a narrow hall, and a fug which he recognised as a vulgarised whiff of her own delicate fragrance.

Her parents came into the hall. The mother filled it. She was a series of graduated tyres, laid flat. The father had an untrained moustache like a small recumbent animal.

'Welcome to the Boon residence.'

'Ard n'a Cushla.'

'He wouldn't have been.' Mrs Boon laughed. With her it was an undertaking, each tyre inflating independently, starting with the pram-size round her neck to the jumbos at her bosom, the Range-Rover round her middle, and finishing at the mini-rings round her ankles.

Meryl slipped her hand into Kevin's, she knew what he was feeling. 'You mustn't mind, it's only their fun. Ard n'a Cushla is the name of our house, called after the place where they spent their honeymoon.'

'I've seen this boy,' said Mr Boon, 'on a ladder outside Marks and Spencers.'

'Kevin works at Dearborn's.'

'It was Marks and Sparks. I never forget a face.'

'Dearborn's are the bathroom people.'

'The M had come off the fascia board. I remember thinking is this a shop that sells arks?'

'I've never seen him,' said Mrs Boon.

'You've never bought a bathroom.' said Meryl.

'You know who he puts me in mind of? Your Aunt Dora.'

'*Dora?*' said Mr Boon.

'It's the widow's peak. Dora's no right to it, she wasn't even engaged.'

'She's got more right to it than he has.' When it was Mr Boon's turn to laugh, his moustache woke up and sported on his lip.

'Kevin works in the office, doing the accounts. He's an accountant.' Meryl hugged his arm, championing him.

'Why are we stood here? I'm not accustomed to keeping visitors in the hall.'

Mr Boon said, 'We're stood here because you're stood there,' and Mrs Boon, moving, revealed the open door of the kitchen where tea was ready. Kevin cheered up at the sight of plates of bread and butter, jam, scones and two kinds of cake.

But Meryl was displeased. 'Here?'

'Why not?'

'Tea in the kitchen?'

Mother and daughter confronted each other. Kevin, unused to close-coupled encounters of this kind, became uneasy. 'I don't mind.'

'There you are then!' Mrs Boon claimed it as a victory.

Mr Boon said, 'My sister Dora is a confirmed spinster. It has led to her being regarded with suspicion and envy.'

'I don't envy her,' said his wife. 'It's not natural for a woman to cut herself off from the best things in life.'

'She runs a successful business.'

'An all-night coffee stall.'

'There's never been anything unnatural in our family.'

'Put the kettle on, Lemmy.' Mrs Boon sat down at the table. Meryl fetched a spoon from the dresser drawer and placed it alongside the jam. Mr Boon, at the cooker, achieved an explosion and a threatening roar. There was a strong smell of gas as he groped for the matches.

'There's always work for a plumber,' said Mrs Boon. 'It's a good trade.'

'I told you, Kevin's an accountant.'

'I expect I'll pick up plumbing,' said Kevin. 'Unit joints and ballcocks and all that jazz.'

'My husband's a fitter. We fit each other.' Mrs Boon expanded as far as her jumbos. Kevin supposed it was mirth she was filling with.

'Sit down,' Meryl said to him. 'You must be tired standing.'

'I'm used to it.' He was in the habit of standing on Saturday afternoons to watch football. Something she couldn't have forgotten.

'Sit down!'

He obeyed. Obviously he had overstepped a mark somewhere.

Mr Boon, having achieved a flame under the burner, left it clawing up the sides of the kettle. 'I watched him with that M. I could see it was heavy. He put it on his shoulder and went up the ladder like a monkey on a stick.'

'That wasn't Kevin!'

'Whoever it was, he was smart.' He lumbered to the dresser and took down a tin with a picture of kittens on it. 'He'd do better with Marks, they've got the best staff conditions.'

'They're Jews,' said Mrs Boon.

'Social Capitalists, the best of both worlds. When you're up that ladder you want to think about sickness benefits. Your father should advise you.'

'His father's dead,' said Meryl.

'I don't know if he is or not,' said Kevin.

'You don't know?'

'He went away.'

'How long for?'

'For ever.'

'A man that can leave his wife and child!' Mr Boon gave a sustained but serious whistle. 'I couldn't do that. I'm not religious but I hang on to a few principles and my own flesh and blood I could never abandon.'

'My mother says it was me he ran away from, he couldn't stand the prospect of a squalling kid.'

'Heathen don't leave their families,' said Mr Boon. 'My feelings are as fine as any heathen's.'

'Kevin has had offers,' said Meryl. 'Boots want him.' It was the first Kevin had heard of it. When he had applied for a job, Boots told him he would be kept in mind should a vacancy occur. 'But he'll probably go into a bank.'

Kevin tried a joke. 'Not me, I prefer to keep my money in the teapot.'

It fell among Boons. Nobody smiled and Kevin was struck with the thought—it gave him quite a knock—that Meryl was also a Boon.

She said sharply, 'He can't stay long, he has another engagement.'

'I have to see my god-uncle.'

'Who?'

'My godfather's brother. He took over when my godfather died.'

'You mean to say you lost your father *and* your godfather?'

'I've got a grandfather.'

'Will he remember you?' said Mrs Boon.

'Grandad can't remember his own name!'

'When he dies I mean, in his will.'

Kevin couldn't see what business it was of hers. She couldn't be looking out for him after a mere five minutes' acquaintance—unless to queer him with Meryl. And if she thought money, or the lack of it, would stop them, she was showing the typical pig-ignorance of parents.

Mr Boon put down the kitten tin and pulled a chair to the table. 'Listen to me, son. Apprentice yourself to a trade that will last. Minis and macros, videos and double-glazing are here today and gone tomorrow. You could find you're an expert on dead ducks by the time you're thirty.'

'There'll always be plumbers,' said Mrs Boon. 'Plumbing's nothing to be ashamed of.'

'I'm not ashamed.'

'Are we ever going to get our tea?' said Meryl.

'Banks are run by computers, there's no future for people in banks.' Mr Boon was a finger wagger. He had fingers like beef sausages, about a pound of them on each arm. He wagged his forefinger at Kevin. 'If you're as smart as Meryl says you are, you'll concentrate on jobs electronics can't do.'

'Make the tea, Lemmy,' said Mrs Boon.

Kevin, to keep his spirits up, debated with himself whether Mr Boon's name could be Lemon: certainly there was something lacking in him.

'Have some bread and butter,' said Meryl.

Kevin said sociably, 'We have a meat tea on Sundays, it's the only day we're both home at teatime.'

'One-parent families are unnatural,' said Mrs Boon. 'They're the cause of all the trouble.'

'What trouble?'

'Vandalism, glue-sniffing, raping old-age pensioners.'

'I'm not a vandal, I don't sniff glue and I wouldn't—' After his recent considerations of the mechanics of sex, Kevin was nauseated—'I wouldn't do anything like that!'

'I'm not saying you would. I'm not saying you haven't

got a good mother. All I'm saying is every boy needs a father.'

'My mother and me don't need anyone.'

'You don't know what she needs.' Mrs Boon glinted like the warning blink of car headlamps.

Mr Boon said, 'I wouldn't want a son of mine to be without a trade in his hands.'

'Kevin's not your son,' said Meryl. Kevin did not miss her sideways glance, it was confederate, it pledged him Meryl herself, and Mr Boon as father-in-law.

'I'm just saying if I had a son. I might have had.'

'Not you,' said Mrs Boon.

'You neither.'

Mr Boon's moustache bristled, Mrs Boon swelled, and Meryl, who was what they had had and ought to be satisfied with, cut herself a piece of cake.

'That jam sponge,' Mrs Boon said to Kevin, 'is pink because one of the eggs had blood in it.'

Sam Spicer, no relative of Kevin's, was an old man of decided views, decided long ago. The only decisions he had to make nowadays were which way to turn his wheelchair and whether to eat his lunch or put it down the lavatory. That sort of existence was killing: Kevin reckoned it was doing for Sam what his blood pressure could do a lot quicker.

He lived in a pensioners' flat with a view of the Athletic Ground. His place was small and nooky and full of old-time furniture with sagging seats and dog legs.

Sam himself poked out of his clothes like a bundle of matchsticks. But he had plenty of colour: purple on his nose, yellow under his eyes and navy blue round his jaw, and he wore a Fair Isle jersey over red and green striped pyjamas.

Kevin, having suffered a deep emotional shock, was glad to find him looking the same as ever. Kevin felt in need of a stabilising element. 'Hi.'

Sam said, 'Huh.'

Kevin was thinking about Nature. The system was deliberately screwed. It took Mr and Mrs Boon to produce Meryl, and now he could see the duplicity behind it. What people meant when they said it was only natural, was that Nature had conned them and there was nothing they could do about it.

Sam drove his wheelchair between the telly and the table, skimming Kevin's shoes. He spent a lot of time practising manoeuvres and was a star performer. He could scorch up to an obstacle and stop a millimetre short. He could bounce down steps and make his tyres yelp as he rounded a corner. He took a walking-stick with him to the shops, pulled down tins from the shelves and fielded them as they fell. Even eggs: he could catch a box of half a dozen if it was properly fastened. There had been misjudgments, but people were indulgent towards a helpless cripple and he enjoyed the risk.

He had been watching a programme in which a lady telly-star described her wild flower window-box. 'That's what I pay my licence for, to hear a silly cow talk about growing dandelions.'

'You don't pay a licence.'

'One of the few benefits of old age.'

'You get all the benefits,' Kevin said gloomily. 'You sit here all day, you don't have to talk to people and you don't have to listen to them.'

'I listen to TV.'

'You can turn it off.'

'I'll tell you when it's nice sitting here. Sunday afternoon is when it's nice. No roast beef and Yorkshire lying on my chest, no washing-up to do. So quiet I can hear a pin drop. If there was someone to drop a pin.'

'Great.'

'No one to interrupt my thoughts when I take a trip down Memory Lane. No legs needed for that. No wheels neither.' Sam spun his chair, hauled it up by its front wheels and balanced it on its hinder ones. 'I used to be a great walker, I never rode if I could walk. This is what I've come to, even my meals are on wheels.'

'I can do that on my bike,' said Kevin. 'I expect it's easier on a bike.'

'It's easier on legs.' Sam let his chair down with a bang. 'The people who've got them don't use them. They go about in rooms.'

'They what?'

'Rooms on wheels. With three-piece suites and radios in them. And cigar-lighters. Nobody walks—left right, left right. Legs drop off if they're not used. How will you like rolling along on your arse?'

'You've got to move with the times.'

Sam burst out laughing, his jersey squeezed in and out of his stomach like a concertina. After a minute Kevin laughed too.

'Mrs Thatcher's times,' said Sam. 'We've got a Queen and that's nice, that's tasteful, she can't do any harm. But a woman Prime Minister!'

'I haven't had a proper tea,' said Kevin.

'There's a Lyons swiss roll.' Sam had a method worked out for whatever he had to do. Nobody could spin a plate across the table like he could. 'My Nellie wouldn't have shop cake in the house. She was a wonderful cook and a sweet girl.' Kevin had seen her photograph and thought she looked like a horse. Sam had married a horse who could cook and he was remembering his sweet horse. 'She was delicate and dainty. She tried to make me dainty.'

'I'm never going to marry.' Kevin was surprised and relieved to hear himself say that.

'I told her I didn't marry to get changed. She had lovely hair, hanging down her back, tied with a bow.'

'A pony tail.'

'She said she had to put it up. I said I like your hair the way it is. "I'm a married woman." she said, "when you marry you have to change." '

'Not on your Nellie.'

The crack just came to Kevin and he thought it was clever, if not brilliant. It was certainly relevant.

But Sam's nose puckered like a dog's. 'You dare say that!'

'I was only joking.'

'You were mocking the dead!'

'No offence meant—'

'I know what was meant. You've got a nasty mind, like all young people nowadays. Only the old have still got their innocence.'

Kevin, to whom innocence was the state of not being with it, wasn't worried for himself. But Sam, leading such a sheltered life couldn't know about people like Mrs Boon. 'This woman I went to see this afternoon was old and she wasn't innocent.'

'How do you know?'

'She puts blood in her cakes.'

Sam swung his chair into reverse and came round the table to Kevin's side. 'I don't like black humour.'

'Black nothing, it's the truth. She happens to be my girl's mother.'

Sam, who had snarled like a dog, now grinned like one. 'And she's teaching her daughter to cook? You'd better learn to like bloody cake.'

'I'm not going to get married.'

'You can't avoid it.'

'I can. I will.'

Kevin cut the swiss roll and took half to the window. Some sort of game was in progress at the Athletic Ground, people running, tangling, falling. He supposed it was football. From up here it looked like a flea circus.

*

How to talk about love? What language to use, plain or pearl, whether to epitomise or capitalise: love as of God, or love the package—a quick warm, like soup in a cup. And in what tense, past or present? Not future, not at my time of life.

I have, always have had, this notion of a gas provided for us to draw on, seize, apportion, stifle in. To me that's love. I gloried in it once, before the advent of Maurice and Melissa. Them I feel for in my bones, I'd have to be disarticulated to stop loving them. The other I remember as a state of highest being. The world came alive, every body, every stone, every breath had the same purpose. It was right and real and had been purposed from the beginning.

Arthur has taken something from his pocket. If he says it's a leaf or a toffee paper I won't ask to see it. A dead mouse I will look at. He says, 'There's someone else,' and holds up a black silk glove.

'What?'

'Another woman.'

I know. Already. It takes no time. I take the glove between my thumb and finger. 'Why is it wet?'

'She dropped it in a puddle.'

'Why?'

'Are you asking why she dropped it?'

'Why did she take it off?'

'Does it matter?'

'Everything matters.' This is the old old story and it has to be told all over again.

'I picked it up and put it in my pocket.'

'And?'

'I forgot it.'

'Is she the one you met on the train? The one I saw you with in the Park?'

'She's never been to the Park.'

'Another one.' I glimpse unimaginable shallows. Why haven't I imagined them? I have imagined everything else. 'When did you pick up the glove?'

'Last night.'

'You were at Rokeby's last night.'

'She works at Rokeby's.'

'What does she do?'

'She operates the word processor.'

She is my enemy, my antithesis: she dazzles and blinds with printed words. 'Is she beautiful?'

'Grow up, Winnie!"

'It's the first question any reasonable woman would ask and you'd better be ready for others. A reasonable woman will ask why do you love this other woman? Why do you think you do? Why aren't I grown up enough for you?'

'I want this straightened out. I hate lying, I've never wanted to deceive you.'

'I know. You want to come out blameless, the instrument of love. An instrument can't be blamed. But we have to take this from the beginning. I'm interested in the time element, I'd like to figure out what I was doing while you were falling in love with somebody else. When did it start?'

'I didn't fall in love.'

'But you make love?'

'Occasionally.'

'What are the occasions? Where? I want to know because it's better to know than to imagine. There are no limits to what I can imagine.' I don't have to tell him that.

'She keeps house for her father, he's a widower. When you think I'm working late at Rokeby's I'm at their place. We have supper and afterwards her father goes to his bowls club. When he leaves the house I leave with him. At the corner of the road we part, he goes one way, I the other. I walk round the block and back to the house. Her father returns home at ten, we have an hour and a half to ourselves. We are free to go upstairs if we wish.' I have an urge to put up my muzzle and howl. 'Sometimes we just sit and talk. Or she plays the piano.'

'What do you talk about while her father is at bowls and the piano is not being played? Politics? Art? Life? Me?'

'Never you.'

He has said to her don't let's talk about Winnie, let's forget her, process me some words of love.

'I want to know what she plays: Mozart, Beethoven, Ketelby? Exercises to strengthen the little fingers?'

'I'm serious about this.'

'So am I. Does she make you wonderful suppers?'

'We usually have a high tea.'

'How high? Eggs scrambled, fried, poached, lightly boiled? Sausage and chips? Steak and mushrooms? Tea can be very high.'

'You're making a game of it.'

'I'm trying to understand. As a reasonable woman would. Or is it too soon for the understanding part? Would a reasonable woman fly into a jealous rage? Weep floods of tears? Break her heart?' That will come later, too late for Arthur. I'll weep when I'm alone.

He says, 'We usually have cold boiled bacon, pickles and cheese.'

'You don't like pickles.'

'Her father does.'

'What's her name?'

'It doesn't matter.'

'It should. It should matter more than anyone else's name. More than mine, mine's not important, except as a place name, the name of a place where you don't want to be.'

'I'm not going to leave you.'

'But you're not going to come to me.'

He senses a meaning which embarrasses him. I didn't intend it at the moment of speaking, but it's relevant.

'It isn't like that.'

'Tell me what it's like. It isn't every man who can boast a word processor as the love of his life.'

'There's no point in going on with this.'

'Linguistically it must be rewarding, you must have greatly enriched your command of words. I'd like to hear you discourse about love.'

If you could see my husband you would appreciate that remark. And, I'm bound to add, if you could see me. You have to see both of us to appreciate it fully. Arthur in his felt boots and droopy cardigan and me with my hair two colours—three, counting the roots— sitting without the telly on, talking about love, romantic love.

But tongue and groove, rock of ages cleft for me is the sort of love I'm thinking about.

IX

ROKEBY, A SUCCESSFUL self-motivator in the business of reprographics and interoffice communication, heard his secretary announce 'Your wife is here.' He dropped his hands over the papers on his desk, a gesture of vexation. He was in the process of preparing an approach with a view to a contract with a multi-national firm of medical suppliers and the question presently occupying him was how medical he should get in the initial stages. 'My wife?'

She was wearing a pink suit which did not make her look frivolous. Frivolity was not one of her traits, she looked over-exposed.

'This is a surprise,' he said. He signed to her to sit in the chair facing his desk, but she did not do so, which was just as well, it would have looked as if he was conducting an interview. 'You didn't tell me you were coming to town.' She had on the little amber necklace her parents had given her on her eighteenth birthday. 'Why don't you wear the thing I bought you?'

'Thing?'

'The pearl rope.' She was out of her element among his anglepoises and laminated finishes: he had never been sure if it was strength or weakness to have such a well-defined element.

He glanced at his watch. 'What are you doing about lunch?' Lunch would present a problem. She ate weird stuff at midday, he doubted if Rudolfo's could run to whole-grain muesli and banana yogurt. 'Let me take you for a decent meal.'

Enid Rokeby, in common parlance an old married woman, was in more precise terms the wife of a wordmonger. Words were his business. Words are freebies, he didn't manufacture, or buy, or go out and kill them. He picked them up and processed them. It was a free enterprise. In personal terms she was a woman of uncertain age, passing but not yet past.

She said, 'I'm leaving.'

'Going shopping?'

'I'm leaving you.'

Rokeby, who had allowed his gaze to return to the papers on his desk, caught sight of the word 'annulment' standing out from the text. Something prickled under his collar. 'What's this?'

'I'm not coming back.'

The door of the office was ajar. He went to it and shut it with his shoulder, stood with his back against it. 'Explain yourself.'

'I've left something for your supper.'

'I wonder at you coming here at a time like this.'

'It seemed like any other time.'

'I'm extremely busy, I have a great deal on hand. I have what could be a *very* great deal.'

'I'm sorry.'

'You think this concentrates my mind?'

'I came to say goodbye.'

The trouble was, he didn't disbelieve her. Anything was possible. 'Are you upset?'

'Not any more.'

'Any more than what?'

'Oh—' Her face fell: she really could let it drop, the next stage was weeping, but she never wept.

She never came to the office either. He recognised an incontrovertible fact when he saw it. 'Something's upset you. We'll go somewhere quiet and you can tell me about it. I'll get Thelma to reserve a table.'

But in the outer office the first thing he saw was her suitcase beside the secretary's desk. He turned back, slammed the door on it. 'What is this? What's going on?'

'I'll collect the rest of my things when I know where I—during the day, when you're not at home—I'll try not to disturb you.'

'Disturb me?' Rokeby caught a glimpse in the actual setting, or re-settling of her face, of the girl she had been. It slipped away immediately out of the corner of his eye. 'What do you suppose you're doing now but disturb me?'

'I'll go.'

'Where?' She shook her head. 'Who's going with you? Naturally there's someone behind this. Who is it? Some man? Or woman? Are you going away with a girl friend?'

'No.'

'So it's a man!'

'No.'

She put a sheltering hand over the amber necklace. If nothing else, she should realise it was too tight for her. The flesh of her neck creamed over it, lightly suffused with pink. Rokeby was visited, unseasonably, by a small organic pang.

His first impulse was to do nothing. She was the offending party and at this stage offence was all that was required of him. He dictated the introductory letter to the medi-company and on second thoughts, rang his friend Walsh.

'I'd like to talk to you.'

'OK, talk.'

'Not over the phone. Meet me at the club at six.'

'Can't it wait?'

'No.'

Walsh called himself a private eye. He managed to feed and maintain himself and an oil-eating Mercedes, and rent an office in the insurance-broker belt of town. Rokeby reasoned that he must know his job.

There was no point in shilly-shallying, he pinned Walsh down with a large whisky. 'Enid's left me.'

'Enid?'

'Unprovoked desertion. I want her tailed.'

'Enid?'

'She's gone to another man.'

'*Enid?*'

'I want to know where she's gone and who with. I'm asking you to find out.'

'I couldn't do that. She knows me, she's known me for years. It was me introduced you to her in the first place.'

'Disguise yourself. Isn't that your job?'

'She'll have gone away for a bit of a change. She'll come back.'

'I don't want her back if I don't know where she's been.'

'What did she say?'

'She said my dinner was in the fridge.'

'Nothing else?'

'She was covering up.'

'*Enid*?'

'You think she's any different from any other woman?' Rokeby was blaming Walsh for raising the question. 'You're a fool if you think that.'

'Then I'm a fool.'

'Are you refusing to help me?'

'I could put Miskin on it.'

'Who?'

'My trainee. It'll be practice for him.'

'Practice be damned, I want a proper job done on her.'

'Never fear, you'll be informed.'

Harvey Miskin's mother had named him after a show she had seen featuring an influential rabbit. So far as Miskin could make out the rabbit had been invisible, which was appropriate to his chosen profession of confidential agent. Till now he had only assisted Walsh with some humble back-up. The Rokeby assignment was his first solo.

'You're on your own,' Walsh said. 'Let's see what you make of it.'

'This is her?'

'This is a snapshot of Mrs Enid Rokeby.'

'It's fuzzy.'

'She doesn't go in for studio portraits. I'll give you a few clues: she uses Chanel No. 5, is wearing a pink suit, is kind to children and animals and is what used to be called a lady.'

'How do I know where to look for her?'

'Use your loaf.'

Miskin, who had faith in his natural assets, decided to start by chatting up Rokeby's secretary.

Thelma was unhelpful, she countered his questions with 'What's it to you?'

'I'm acting on behalf of Mr Rokeby.'

'He's never said anything to me.'

'He wouldn't, would he? His wife running off and leaving him is a delicate matter.'

'Delicate? Him?'

'Anything you say will be treated as strictly private and confidential. It's Mrs Rokeby I'm interested in. Do you know where she may have gone?'

'I wouldn't tell you if I did.'

Miskin was not without guile. He groaned, dropped into a chair, hung his bony wrists out of his sleeves. 'That finishes me. My first job and I've fluffed it.'

'Prying and spying, what sort of job's that?'

'Helping people can't be wrong.'

'It depends what you call helping.'

'Supplying information is a service. Sorting out problems, settling people's worries. Wouldn't you rather know than be kept in the dark?'

'No.'

'Well, it doesn't matter. I've failed to get any sort of lead, obviously I'm not cut out for the work. It's back to the job creation schemes.'

'I suppose you've got an old mother to support.'

'And a wife and six children.' Miskin stood up, sighing. 'Been nice talking to you.'

'I don't know where she went, but I know where she was going.' Miskin waited, not allowing himself too much hope. 'She left here in such a hurry she forgot her case and rang through from Paddington. She couldn't face coming back to collect it, so I offered to take it to her in my lunch hour.'

'That was kind.'

'She gave me my taxi fare and something for my trouble.

She's thoughtful, I'll say that. She said she could catch the Weston train if she hurried.'

'Weston?'

'Super-Mare. Super sea. Not horse.'

Miskin restrained himself. Remember, he thought, you're dealing with women, sex does count, in more than the one way.

The lead was slender. Just how slender he began to realise when he got to Weston. It was the end of the season, people moved fretfully between the fish-diners and fun-parlours, seeking shelter and solace. A few sat in the public gardens where work had started on digging up the annuals and putting in Spring bulbs. There were enough people to make his task difficult, not enough to let him off the hook. He might waste a lot of time on reasonable hope, and hope was worse than fat chance.

He turned away from the town, looked at the bay. The big nothing out at sea and a squall of rain drove him inland. He stood in Marks and Spencer's watching it, and felt like Maigret. With a lead like this Maigret would light his pipe and put his mind to the matter of Mrs Rokeby, a woman fed-up or frightened, happy or unhappy, in a pink suit or the arms of a lover. Where would such a woman go in Weston-Super-Mare?

It occurred to Miskin that he had been sent on a fool's errand, the idea being to show him that he wasn't up to the job. Walsh had said that fieldwork required special attributes and that it remained to be seen whether Miskin had them. Miskin could call this the remainder.

The rain wasn't Maigret's, it was swilling in fried-egg-shaped bubbles along the gutters. Weston-Super-Rain. Miskin turned to face into the big bright Marks and Sparks. The sensible thing would be to have a meal and take the next train back. Walsh would not be surprised. Walsh, sod him, would expect it.

A man was examining a lady's nightdress. He lifted the hem, put his fist under it, looked at his knuckles through the flimsy material. Miskin was reminded of something

Walsh was fond of saying about having to decide where sin ends and crime starts. He felt he was about to understand it when he saw Mrs Rokeby, bold as brass, bold as a stick of pink peppermint rock.

He took the snapshot out of his pocketbook, studied it, and her. He went close, close enough to see the rain spots on her suit. In profile she looked beakier.

She was holding up a dress, considering it, with her head on one side, smiling the self-same smile as in the snapshot. A woman who could smile that same smile in a garden at whoever was photographing her, and in a superstore at a dress which she might or might not buy, could hide anything. But give or take a fuzz or two, she was the woman in the snapshot. And the dress department of a superstore was where she would conceivably go if she needed something nice to wear, or to pass an hour while she waited for Mr X.

Jubilant, he kissed the photograph. Then he told himself now you've got to go to work and prove she's who you think she is.

Tailing her would be easy. Obviously she didn't have a mackintosh with her, and the pink suit would twinkle all the way. He waited for her to make a move, which she did, to a mirror. Holding the dress in front of her, she put one hand on her hip, did a little twirl. It was a dark red dress with a scoop neck and would suit her. She smiled at Miskin in the mirror. He ducked, adopting the old dodge of tying his shoelace while watching her feet.

They were nice narrow feet with high insteps, she wore black silk stockings, sheer, so that her ankle-bones shone through. Miskin took note, it was his job. The feet moved back to the dress-rail. She took down another dress, went through the same performance, carrying it to the mirror, draping it against herself, smiling the smile. Miskin went over to the perfumery where a salesgirl sought to interest him in an after-shave called 'Blue Movie'. 'It's a fun smell, you'll be tickled pink.' On the word 'pink' Mrs Rokeby walked away. Miskin followed. He had practised tailing and to make his task more difficult had always chosen someone routine, the sort who mingled and was easily lost sight of. He had become quite slippy at taking cover, at educated guesswork, making himself invisible. He wasn't called Harvey for nothing.

Mrs Rokeby offered no challenge. She was a shopper, not a buyer. She wandered from department to department of the supermarts, from window to window of smaller shops. Her eye was caught by everything. Miskin could have stayed at her elbow because not once did she look round. The pink suit printed itself on his eyeballs.

It wouldn't have been so tedious if she had been looking for something—a toothbrush she had forgotten to bring, a gift for Mr X, a steak for supper, aspirin, a three-piece suite. But she was looking for the sake of looking, to pass the time. Till it was time for the assignation. She was going to it slowly.

Miskin started cutting corners and instead of tailing her through ladies' lingerie to videos, he lurked within sight of the exits. Then she fooled him, she left via soft furnishing, came round a side street and looked straight through him.

After that he kept her in sight and when she finally drifted into a coffee-bar he went in after her.

She was at a table by the window, looking out. She had a thing about windows, it told Miskin something about her state of mind. It meant she needed glass to look through and protect her. She couldn't decide between Mr Rokeby and Mr X: one had the money, the other had the charm—probably that was all he had. Miskin was glad his business was this side of the glass, though it wouldn't have taxed any normal intelligence to advise her. There was still time to buy the red dress and take the train back to London. It would be easy for her, she only need tell the truth: 'I've been such a fool, can you forgive me?' and turn on the kittenry.

'Are you following me?'

She was beside him, looking at him—and not through

glass. She sat down at his table, smiling the smile. He told himself to act the dummy and stared, not forgetting while he had the chance, to observe her face at close range. There were stretch marks round her mouth, a scribble of red veins on each cheekbone. But this was the face in the snapshot he carried in his breast pocket. Mrs Enid Rokeby. 'I think you were,' she said.

'Were what?'

'There's something I can do about it you know, and it wouldn't be what you want.' Miskin thought if she called the police he would run for it. 'You were spying on me. Very clumsily, I must say.'

'Not me.'

'A Churchill tank could do it better.'

Miskin had scarcely heard of a Churchill tank but he took the meaning. 'Why should I spy on you? I don't know you.' He reflected that she couldn't know him, and suggested buying her a coffee.

He was prepared for her to try to slip away while his back was turned, but when he brought the coffee to the table she was tipping coins out of her purse. He said, 'This on me.'

'Thank you.'

'This is my first time in Weston and I've been looking round. Like you.'

'Is that what I've been doing?'

'You must have been, or you wouldn't have seen me. It's not such a super place, is it? The sea's no better than at Brighton. Not so good, in fact. I like the noise it makes under the pier at Brighton when it pulls back on the pebbles.' She started messing with her coffee, dipping into it with the spoon as if she expected to find something. 'And the town's not much. Give me King's Road.'

'I like it here.'

'Or Charlton Park,' he said boldly. Charlton Park was where the Rokebys lived and he watched her like a hawk, all his senses alert. As he spoke the name he caught a whiff of her perfume. Chanel No. 5. He had taken the trouble to go and sniff it in Boots. 'Charlton Athletic's home ground. What do you find that's so special about this place?'

'Memories.' She flicked her plastic spoon which bounced across the table and fell to the floor. 'I came here for my honeymoon.'

Miskin nodded sagely. 'Cheers you up to go somewhere you've been happy.'

'Who said anything about happy?'

'Oh, sorry.'

'You needn't be. You didn't marry me. Have you got a light?'

'Sorry—' Nothing had been said about her smoking.

'Never mind, it's a Job's comforter. I was your age when I married, the daft age. Speaking for myself, naturally.' She gave him a big smile, showing her teeth which were good. 'I'm sure you're very sensible. I was just a silly kid.'

'It took two of you, didn't it?'

'Let's say happiness is egg-shaped and we cracked it.'

'Are you staying here long?'

'As long as I can have some fun.'

'Fun?'

She put an unlit cigarette in her mouth and looked along it, focussing him. His skin crept. 'I'd like a little joy in my life.'

'Wouldn't we all? My name's Harvey, by the way. What's yours?'

'Sherryzaday.'

'What?'

'That's by another way.'

If he knew why she was joshing him, because of his age or his approach—but she had made the approach, hadn't she?—he wouldn't mind so much. 'I'm here on business, a flying visit. Here today, gone tomorrow. Haven't yet booked in at a hotel. Do you know a good one?'

'They're full up where I'm staying.' She dropped the

unsmoked cigarette into her coffee. 'You know what I'd like? A drink.'

Miskin had no option but to follow her out. They went through the rain to a place fitted up like a Spanish galleon.

'My shout,' she said. 'What will you have?'

'Lemon shandy.'

The other thing to remember was to keep a clear head. He thought she called the barman 'Harry', but when she brought the drinks she said, 'Don't you hate this sort of thing?'

'What sort?'

'Gimmickry. Hurricane lamps and doubloon beer-mats. Things made out to be what they're not.'

'In our park at home they've planted a flowerbed that looks like a clock. No sense in it, it can't tell the time.'

'The Bible says: "God hath chosen things which are not to bring to naught things which are".' Miskin thought that nobody had bothered to warn him she was religious. 'I hate deception. It's been my luck to get involved with people who pretend to be what they're not.'

She was watching Miskin, seeing through him. Let her: all he had to hide was Rokeby, he had pretended only to himself, he hadn't claimed an identity or told her any lies. He asked point-blank, 'What's the name of your hotel?'

'Why do you want to know?'

'Because if it's full up I won't go there looking for a bed.'

'I hoped you might.' She left him and went to the bar for another drink.

He opened his mind a little. She could be giving Rokeby a tough time, needling, moralising and quoting from the Bible. 'She's what used to be called a lady', Walsh had said, and Rokeby, the little Miskin had seen of him, looked like an ageing barrow-boy. But it was no part of his job to sort out their differences.

She brought him another shandy, herself a large gin. He said, 'I should be paying.'

She said, 'Two pounds ten pence.' Miskin groped for

his wallet. 'Idiot.' She put her hand on his chest, suddenly she was soft-voiced and womanly. 'Tell me about yourself.'

'I'd rather hear about you.'

'That's a silly story.'

'I shan't laugh.'

'My husband didn't like being touched.' She splayed her five fingers on his shirt, as if picking out a tune.

'Is he dead?'

'I shouldn't think so. He's strong and healthy. That's what first attracted me, his health and strength. And he married me to prove it. You don't mind being touched?'

'Of course not.'

'He goes cold when I touch him.'

'Cold hands, warm heart.'

'His heart's like a bullock's, nothing in it but blood.'

Her eyes, looking into his, had gone blue-black and inky. She was morbid, and with that, as well as what else he had discovered her to be, she added up to quite a handful. He didn't even know if Rokeby wanted her back. But he was getting the picture, he was the central figure in it. Walsh had despatched him with a minimum of information so that he should make a complete cock-up. Walsh had never been encouraging, had consistently held him back, saying he wasn't ready for fieldwork, doubted if he was the right material.

She said, 'I said it was a silly story.'

'I'm not laughing.'

'Would you like to see me to bed?'

Being lucky helped, Walsh couldn't take that away. 'I'll walk you to your hotel.'

'Can you afford it? I charge by the hour for coming up. Payment in advance.'

Rokeby's wife Enid did not share his concern with words. She was often at a loss for them. When they were first married he took pleasure, loving and mischievous, in supplying her with right and wrong ones. That amusement palled, and now they communicated on a modified basis. The element of hit or miss tended to liven things up between them. Enid was predictable, not to say—as her husband he was entitled to say it—dull. Her idea of an interesting conversational topic was the fluctuation in prices at Sainsbury's. He had taken to supplying her meaning without waiting for her to state it. Time was saved, and patience.

'I can't go on,' she had said, the day before she left. 'I'm so tired—'

It made him angry when she talked about being tired as if she was a skivvy working herself to the bone. 'For God's sake get someone to help you. Get a woman.'

'A woman?'

'Or a girl, an au-pair, get an au-trio if you like. We can afford it.'

She didn't finish what she was saying either because she had forgotten what she wanted to say, or because she hadn't known in the first place.

He was thinking, as he waited for Walsh, that there was no mystery. Walsh was coming to report to him where she had gone and what had become of her. Rokeby saw very well what she would become: a fly on the wall, too frightened to move, with no notion where flies go in the wintertime.

A woman alone, what did she expect? That last morning she had blundered out of his office as if there was a broom behind her, going, going, gone. Without expectations. He had some, though. A woman alone, a woman like her—Getting up suddenly from his desk he collided with the wastebin. Its contents shot out over the carpet.

His staff had gone, the cleaner was vacuuming in the outer office. He opened the door and shouted to her. She didn't hear, he had to go and tap her on the shoulder. She nearly jumped out of her skin: he thought it would have been an improvement, she didn't look as if she often washed.

When she switched off the Hoover, dust puffed up from the bag. 'That bag needs emptying,' he said.

'You gave me a turn, I didn't know anyone was in there. That's the boss's office—Rockabye's.'

'Rokeby. I am he.'

'Are you so? I'm Mrs O'Flynn. Pleased to meet you.' She held out her hand.

'Oblige me by picking up the mess in my office.'

'You never stay till this time. Behind with your work are you?'

'No, and I'd rather you weren't behind with yours.'

'There's no rush.' She leaned on the Hoover. 'Nothing to do upstairs now the engravers have shut down. Their business was bad. How's yours?'

'We'll survive.'

'I do all the offices in this block and this one's the nicest. It's got style. I like the green plants, green's relaxing.' Propped on the Hoover she looked thoroughly relaxed. 'You're not. I should've thought you would be.'

Rokeby was irritated to find himself a disappointment to Mrs O'Flynn. He went into his office, was careful to tread in and re-scatter the contents of the wastebin. 'Clear this up, please.'

'You're a bit after the style of Mr P at P and Q's. Heavy-built, always on the go so he is. But you haven't got a heart.'

'What do you mean?'

'I can see you haven't. You've none of that nasty blue round the lips and you don't heave like a bellows. You should be glad you haven't got a heart.'

She was starting to pick up the paper when Walsh arrived. Rokeby pushed him into the outer office and shut the door on her. 'Tell me what you've found out and keep your voice down.'

'I wasn't going to shout.'

'There's an old witch on the Hoover listening in.'

'You'll be glad to know it's not what you thought.'

'If anyone else tells me to be glad I'll make them sorry.'

'I thought you'd like to know she hasn't run off with someone.'

'Where's she gone? And why?'

'Weston-Super-Mare. For no ascertainable reason, except that you went there for your honeymoon.'

'We didn't, we went to Torquay.'

'Well, she's at Weston, alone, at a non-star hotel.'

'You mean to say she forgot where we went for our honeymoon?'

'We're not mind-readers. I suggest you ring up and talk to her. Or better still, go to Weston and talk.'

'What about?'

'Sweet-talk her. Say you miss her and want her back.'

'I'm no good at it, my business is with facts.'

'This isn't business.'

'Is that all you can tell me?'

'It's up to you what you do with it.'

'What can I do if I can't get through to her?'

'Try saying it with flowers.'

'You think she'll listen to a bunch of chrysanthemums?'

'Make it red roses, they're supposed to mean a loving heart.'

*

They say we aren't talking face to face, we can no longer switch moods or watch for reactions, our decisions pop up on visual display screens and our messages are squawked out over Tannoy systems. In business, in hospitals, in shops, out of our own pockets, the electronics are reaching to us, coming from people we've never seen or touched. We're being dehumanised.

But there's nothing new about cutting yourself off from genuine emotion. Saints have done it: tyrants, witches, bomber pilots did it; nuclear scientists, soap operas and the wonder of Woolies do it. But now they blame technology. We're into podism. People are becoming pods. And don't think of a nice fat row of peas, because the pods are empty, no passion, no warmth, no milk of human kindness. No humans. Remote control and telecommunications are making pods of us all.

Personally, I wouldn't mind losing some genuine emotion. I'm full of the basics, wall-to-wall with fear, jealousy, rage, hope, guilt, most kinds of love. I'd welcome a few free areas, a fresh through-draught. Every day I'm washing and cooking and hoping things will turn out to be better than I think they are.

I have a husband, a nice home, two lovely children but there's still room for improvement. Yesterday I made animal cookies for my daughter and she wouldn't eat the camel because it had only one hump. Each time I fold up my nightdress, I think what's wrong with me, I'm WX but I've seen bigger stomach bulges on schoolgirls.

A change is coming. I shan't have a husband, Arthur will be my tied tenant. I shall have my nice home—at least it'll be where I still live and where my lovely children will live until they're ready to leave.

It will be podism of a sort, so I suspect I'll get my wish, the way we usually get our wishes—screwed.

I've been asked to America to tell my stories to colleges, theatre groups, sororities and mature student classes. They call me the English Phenomena.

'Phenomenon. With an 'a' it's plural,' says Angie.

'With an 'a' it's feminine. They're planning State-wide hook-ups, I'll be a nine days' wonder.'

'Shall you like that?'

'I never expected to go down into history. I'm not an innovator: the Canterbury pilgrims and that Persian woman, Scheherezade, were before me. But I'll reach a lot of people in nine days.'

'What will you tell them?'

'It will depend on things which aren't known to me yet. I've got it all in me and it's bound to come out.'

'When did it start to come out?'

I tell her once upon a time, the time before this, when software was ladies' lingerie and hardware was saucepans.

'Your formative years,' she says, writing it down.

'The girlie magazines were for girls, they carried free trial offers of silk-sifted face-powder in three lovely shades.'

Angie wants to know what shades.

'Rachel, Peachbloom and Moonlight. I used to mix them together to get biscuit-beige which was about right for my complexion.'

'Which magazines did you read?'

Angie has her pencil ready, she is interested. Professionally.

'I was on the publishing staff. Like you.'

'I wonder at you choosing a job in publishing when you don't like seeing words on paper.'

'As you said, they were my formative years, I was getting formed. I made the tea and stuck down the envelopes, a couple of hundred a day. I licked them all, it helped take the coating off my tongue.' Angie shudders. 'I had no interest in the mill-girl romances and demon-lover stuff they were publishing. But I got to know some writers.'

They didn't fit into my conception of class. They had a streak which made them fall short of being ladies and gentlemen, it was a high cunning, nothing to do with culture, and a lot tougher. They had the advantage of me and they let me see when they didn't take it. Theirs was a closed community. It had to be, to sustain the illusions they were dealing in. I was an outsider.

The office building was a converted hotel, I sat in what had been one of the bathrooms. It had a spaghetti junction of pipes which hammered like mad whenever a lavatory was flushed somewhere else in the building. The next door office had been the salon of the bridal suite and was occupied by the editorial staff, two men and two women. They contributed to the magazine: the men taking it in turn to write the cliffhangers and the children's page, the women doing 'Nurse Nightingale—help with your personal problems', and 'Ramona, features and fortune'.

The editor-in-chief had his headquarters in what had been the bridal chamber, there were cupids all over the ceiling. He was dedicated. At the editorial meetings every hackneyed plot and wonted emotion brought stars or tears to his eyes. I never could tell if it was because he was vulnerable or disgusted.

One other member of staff occupied what was once a pantry and was called the Bookroom because the bound copies of past issues of the paper were kept there. He was an Anglo-Indian by the name of Plonn. He typed like a machine gun, writing under various pseudonyms—Bettina Bellair, Deirdre Ford-Maddox, Laura Ravelstoke. He made a point of noticing me. No one else did.

Nurse Nightingale smoked fifty cigarettes a day and remembered my existence only when she ran out of Craven A. Between Glenda Greytower and Sally Jukes— the two men—was fierce competition. They were too taken up with in-fighting to bother with me. But Plonn would leave whatever he was doing and give me his whole attention.

At first I was grateful, but I soon wearied of his jokey manner. He teased me mercilessly—I see that now. He knew I was unhappy and he was trying to push me into the circle. But he went the wrong way about it.

Every week there was a meeting in the editor's office to discuss future issues. I had no shorthand and could type only with one finger, so my presence was not required until teatime. Nurse Nightingale took notes and everyone was expected to come up with sparkling new ideas. 'Sparkling' was a word they used a lot: 'sparkling new' was the highest praise. Sally Jukes and Glenda Greytower fought for it. Nurse Nightingale didn't qualify, what with pimples being mucky and real sex still under wraps. Ramona sparkled when she chose.

Plonn wrote romances about nice girls and intrepid men. The editor praised his stories for their old-fashioned flavour. Plonn passed most of the meeting doing the *Telegraph* crossword. But when I took round the tea he asked what was it—Ceylon, Assam or Darjeeling. I said I didn't know.

'Should we ennoble it with the name of tea when it is undoubtedly the sweepings from under native feet? Bearing in mind the afflictions of native feet—button scurvy, jiggers, black toe, and their predilection for being naked, and the fact that sacred cows are no more sanitary then secular ones—'

'Shut up, Plonn,' said Sally Jukes.

'I'm urging our young friend always to give thought to the nature of things, in this instance the ingredients of her cups of char.'

'They're not mine,' I said, 'they're from the Home and Colonial.'

At sixteen I wasn't prepared to laugh at myself and I complained about him to Ramona. She was making up her mouth. She drew a scarlet rosebud and kissed the air. 'Plonn's an old goat but he's not a fumbler. You're quite safe.'

'I don't like the way he talks.'

She slipped a tissue between her lips, lightly compressed them and tossed the rosy stain into the wastebin. It was an operation I admired and envied. 'You'll be lucky if you never hear worse.'

She fascinated me. I was at the age to covet people. I longed to be her, a pretty, self-assured young woman with a lovely perm, full make-up, chunky jewellery and Russian boots. I didn't care how much I might lose of my life or my nature, I would gladly have lost it all if I could have stepped inside her skin.

I said, 'I love your nails.' She held them up, all scarlet ten. I said, 'They really do sparkle.'

I can recall her facial expressions to this day. They weren't all that varied, she didn't have great scope with Nurse Nightingale and the two men. She was often bored. I remember her frowning, knitting her smooth white brow into lilac shadows, and her brilliant smile which came and went like sunshine. What I didn't like to see was her discontent. I thought surely she has everything, I thought it was possible to have everything and live. It was my own chances I was reckoning: if she, with all her advantages, wasn't satisfied, what hope had I?

One day she said 'Stop mooning round with your tongue out.' She spoke without looking up from her desk. I shut my mouth. I have that habit when I'm taking in someone or something. I look and listen, and try to taste.

Nurse Nightingale said, 'The kid's crazy about you.'

'How dare you.' The words came into my head and I was pleased with the dignified way I spoke them.

Nurse Nightingale gave one of her smoker's laughs. 'Don't worry, kiddy, you're normal.'

'I'm not crazy about anyone!'

'It's Nature's way of preparing you for adult sex.'

My dignity collapsed. I shouted. 'I'm not! I never!' I approached Ramona who was powdering her nose. 'You don't believe it—you know it's not true!'

'Go away and make the coffee.' She snapped her compact shut and snapped me in two.

I was sixteen and had never been prone to schoolgirl crushes. I examined myself to see whether I could be getting them late in life. I took the idea of all-female sex as far as my technical knowledge allowed, and was put right off. I daren't look Ramona in the face, but that was no problem because she didn't look into mine.

Nurse Nightingale continued to treat with me when she wanted cigarettes or baked jam-roll brought up from the dairy. Those two just weren't interested. I had to accept that if they thought of me at all it would be as a silly little freak. I wasn't even sure if I was important enough to be passed round as the office joke, who else was or was not thinking of me in those terms. I was not equipped to cope with a negative situation. I brooded, thinking of ways to make myself felt, make them all sit up begging my forgiveness and not getting it. I wanted Ramona with her face in a mess and Nurse Nightingale burned down like one of her cigarette ends. But there was nothing I could do except try to look normal.

Plonn was the only one who treated me as something

more than a piece of office furniture and he continued to have fun with me. It was his own brand, not shared with the others, which was a small mercy. But I wasn't grateful.

He would call me into his room, the old pantry, stuffed floor to ceiling with bound copies of the paper which smelled. They would, wouldn't they, they went back to 1922 when women wore crinolines. Plonn had a smell too: I go back into it whenever I go into a public bar. I feel like I did then—endangered.

He knew I was lonely, I daresay he was too, but he had learned to do without people and I hadn't. He kept trying to reach me.

'So you want to be a writer,' he'd say, as if I had just said I did.

'No.'

'Like Ruby M. Ayres and Virginia Woolf.'

'No.'

'No to Ruby or no to Virginia?'

'I don't want to be a writer.'

'Not even a Bettina Bellair? You're the only person ever to come into this dream world without the sordid intention of making money.' He crooked his finger but I refused to go closer. 'Tell me, Winnie—no, I can't call you that, it doesn't suit you. I'll call you Moon Tiger.'

'I'm not a moon nor a tiger.'

'Don't you like it? It's the name of something rather pretty and very useful in the Far East. A little contrivance that glows the night through and keeps mosquitoes away. So what do you want to do?'

'Nothing.'

'Like the grasshopper and the bee? I fear you will be obliged to make some gesture of counter-productivity just to show that you're having fun. The grasshopper had to hop grass which could be just as wearing as the bee's industry.'

'It wasn't a bee, it was an ant.'

I always felt better if I could exit on a winning line.

One morning when I went in with the post I found

him slumped over his desk. I approached cautiously on creaking shoes. He was making a noise between a gargle and a sigh, he seemed to be asleep.

I looked down at his brown onion-skin, the black pores on his nose, the fuzz in his ears and the shine where his scalp showed through his hair. Uncharitable, I missed nothing.

One of the bound volumes lay open on his desk. It smelled old. His desk drawer stood ajar. Inside was a bottle of something. Whisky, I decided, with the contempt of the unenlightened. His cheek was pillowed on the page of typescript still in the machine. Words caught my eye: 'her hand fluttered to her breast—that little white hand like a frightened dove . . .'

'Bah!' I said, and then by a chance in a thousand, for there must have been a thousand words on the printed page, I saw the words again: 'her hand fluttered to her breast, that little white hand like a dove . . .'

Plonn's head covered most of his typed sheet but I picked up a couple more sentences word for word the same as those in the bound volume. *Love's Errantry* the story was called. The bound copies were those for the first quarter of 1925.

At sixteen plagiarism was unknown to me, I'd have said you could steal anything from a kiss to the Crown Jewels. Words were anybody's.

Plonn roused himself with an extra loud gargle and sat up, licking his lips as if he was tasting something nasty. It took him a minute to get me into focus.

'Ah, the grasshopper—come to mock the bee.'

'I brought your post.'

'This poor old bee toiling to produce his stint of honey.'

'You were asleep.'

'I was collecting my thoughts. I don't like the look of some of them so it's best done with my eyes shut.'

'It was an ant. And hands aren't like doves.' That stopped him. He chewed on something. I said, 'A hand can't be frightened.'

'In my little story it is.'

'What's errantry?'

'Roving, wandering. It stems from the Latin *errare*. Love's a wanderer and the biggest blunderer of all. Wouldn't you say so?' He tapped the open page of the volume. 'You've been peeping, like the wizards in the Bible that peeped and muttered. Shall you mutter?' He sighed. 'You've been looking at literary history. This story—all the stories in these old numbers—are fairy tales of their time. They were written in the age of innocence, the blossoming of romance after the dark satanic mills of the Industrial Revolution. When tenderness was a known quantity. We shall not see their like again.'

I didn't know what he was talking about. I was suffering from the combined smell of the old books and his breath. I edged towards the door.

'Come here, Tiger—or is it Moon? Moon of my delight. So many lovely girls in my life—' He tried standing, swayed, and dropped back in his chair. 'I want you to understand what I'm doing here, I'm bringing these old sweet stories to life. I am a resurrectionist. You think that's a simple operation, a mere matter of copying.' He stared at me and I stared back, vexed that he should suppose I was thinking about his silly old stories. 'In fact it's a specialised task, requiring expertise and complete sympathy with the genre. Which I happen to have. Stories like these are an enchantment. They cannot be dragged by the scruff into modern times, they must be prepared, adjusted, balanced, toughened. Even—I have to say it—sullied, to suit our vulgar taste. A story's not alive unless it's told.'

I said I thought I was about to be sick.

'Put your head between your knees—No, better not, that's for fainting.' He brought the bottle out of the desk drawer. 'A little brandy will settle your stomach. No? Ah well, it will settle mine. I must ask you not to mention this episode to anyone. Let it be our secret. The idea of resurrecting these romances is my own entirely. I'm about to take out a patent. You may not know it, but people covet the creative spirit and they will steal it from under your nose.' He sucked the last drops out of the bottle. It didn't do anything for him, his eyeballs rolled like a dog's expecting a beating. 'The truth is, I can no longer write the bloody stuff. A guinea a thousand's not much but if I don't get it I don't drink.' I thought I shouldn't have been told, it was an imposition. He said, 'I'm drinking myself to death, Tiger, and I must have the money to finish the job.'

Angie nods and writes: 'A story's not alive unless it's told.' She says, 'I'd like something about your early life—'

'I was told I was a wet baby.'

'—for the profile.'

'Be sure to show my best side.'

'I can't promise anything. It depends on what my editor thinks our readers will want to read.'

'Whatever happened to truth?'

She giggles. 'Oh that.'

'I don't care what your readers want. I live other people's lives. Professionally.'

'So do writers.'

'Writers deal in artefacts. The spoken word came before paper and ink. Do you know, when I was a kid I thought biscuits were broken on principle, to make you aware you were eating a luxury. We couldn't afford whole ones. We did our shopping on Saturday nights when the perishables were sold cheap. My clothes came from church jumbles, my mother's from the houses where she worked as a daily help.'

Angie sighs. 'That's old stuff, it really creaks.'

'We were really poor. We couldn't afford to buy a skewer of horsemeat for our cat.' That word 'really—reelly—raally' prinks about and means nothing. 'One winter the only coat my mother had was a velvet evening wrap trimmed with swansdown. It looked nice but it didn't keep out the cold. When she went out at night—on business she said, I believed her then but now I know what her business was—I worried about her. Have you any idea what it means for a child to worry about an adult? It's the tortoise worrying about the hare.

'My mother did what she had to without shame, i.e. buying scrag ends and broken biscuits and that other business which she made fun. Shame's a sort of worry, isn't it? She took everything as it came, never looking over the top. That's the child's prerogative, the acceptance world. Or ought to be. I lost mine when Father Christmas caught fire.

'My mother had a blithe spirit. It was invincible and shone even through her clothes, especially through the blue velvet wrap. Sometimes she came home blue all over. Like the Ice Maiden. I worried about her not having a warm coat and she said there were more ways than one of keeping warm.'

Angie says she can't put that in, it's open to wrong interpretations. She asks was I happy at school.

'I was popular because I came bottom in everything, which meant that no one else could so they all felt safe with me.'

'Were you punished?'

'Whacked, you mean? Detained? They could have beaten me black and blue and kept me in for a month, it wouldn't have been any use. I had a natural resistance to being educated. Teachers said I was a bad influence and put me at the back of the class. Everyone loves a bad influence. It's important to come somewhere in people's estimation and better to come low than high because then you don't disappoint.'

Angie looks owlish. 'You delight millions.'

'Do I delight you?'

'Well, I haven't actually—but I've read about your sessions all over the country. The reception you get beats anything the Beatles had.'

'People were more inhibited in those days.'

'I wonder how your schoolfriends think of you now.'

If they think at all they think of the day a big girl

accosted me in the playground. It was bound to happen because my clothes came from jumble sales. Angie says that creaks, so I shan't tell her.

The girl pointed to the dress I was wearing, a clanless tartan with a neckline that showed my clavicle. 'That's mine,' she said.

'It's not.'

'It is so.'

I didn't like the dress but I was ready to defend my right to wear it. 'It is not yours!'

'I can prove it. There's the green button we sewed on because we didn't have a red one.

'That doesn't prove anything.'

'Anyone can see it's not your size.'

'My mother bought it big so I can grow into it.'

'My mother sent it to the jumble,' said the big girl, 'and that's where your mother bought it.'

'Jumble!' said someone.

They joined hands, chanted 'Win, Win, gets her clothes from the jumble bin.'

I tried to escape but they made a circle round me and I couldn't break out.

'Winnie-ninny in her secondhand pinny!'

What made it worse was their good nature. They were smiling, even the girl whose dress it had been and always would be.

I laid violent hands on it, tore it off. A daft thing to do. In my liberty bodice and knickers I was a comical sight. There was a moment of silence, then someone laughed.

'That's my liberty bodice!'

'Those are my knickers!'

They fell about laughing. And what did I do? I stripped off the rest of my clothes. No tease, in blind rage I tore at the buttons and threw my liberty bodice in their faces. I shoved my bloomers over my ankles and kicked them high over their heads. Their laughter stuck in their throats, they stared, wide-eyed.

Before they or I could make another move, there sounded the blast of a whistle and the teacher taking playground duty was upon us.

I was sent home with a letter accusing me of morbid exhibitionism. My mother asked me what I had done.

'I took my clothes off.'

'Like mother, like daughter,' she said, and *she* laughed.

This is another time. Arthur and I, tellyless, are trying to talk about love. Again. I started it. 'Why don't you go and live with her?' It was a serious suggestion, and cost me to make, but I don't like to see him tired and dispirited. 'Why should three of us be unhappy when one will do?'

'One?'

'I'm afraid I can't undertake to rejoice, but there's no need for you and—what's her name?'

'She isn't unhappy. She has her work, her home, her father, her music. She has a full life.'

You should never laugh at a statement like that. He could say the same about me. 'She doesn't have you.'

'She doesn't want me to that extent.'

'What is her extent? I'm not being prurient, I want to know what your relationship is. You must see that it matters.'

'She's someone I can talk to.'

He has taken us past the weeping post. I may weep for lost love, but not for lost conversation. Yet it hurts as much. It has a pain threshold which goes back to Mrs McSweeny and the crucifixion. 'What can you talk to her about?'

'Anything.'

'You said that before. Give me an idea of your topics.'

'Why?'

'Well obviously they will include things you can't talk to me about. Or think you can't. I wish you'd try me— I'll listen and you talk and we'll see what I make of it. Whether it's the same as she does.'

It's her fault that he's tired, mine that he's dispirited. This is how I must expect him to be when he's with me. I don't know what he's like when he's with her. Inspirited and sparkling? An hour and a half is long enough to sparkle after he's done a day's work and he isn't getting younger.

'Do you talk about the children? Yours and mine?'
'Sometimes.'
'Does she wish they were yours and hers?'
'I shouldn't think so.'

With what he knows about women he wouldn't think so. What any man knows about women doesn't include the Mother Earth thing. But she'll be thinking that Maurice and Melissa could be hers. Her unborn children.

'Perhaps I could talk to her too and she could translate—we've got to the stage where we need an interpreter.'

'Be reasonable,' he says, hanging on the word, and I see what a lovely word it is, sweet and strong and womanly.

'I'm trying. I have to ask your reasons because I don't have any. Not for this—this girl—who's happy with her music and her home and her word processor.'

'Could we leave it?' He closes his eyes.

'Till some other time? When you're not tired? Sunday morning?'

The phone rings, he gets up to answer it.

'Oh hullo!' he cries, welcoming. 'Of course not, we were only chatting. No, she isn't here. Melissa was off school this afternoon with a sore throat. She hasn't been out since lunchtime. You're worried?—Don't panic, kids have stomach clocks and it's not teatime yet.—I know, you can't be too careful. Look, if she hasn't turned up within the hour I'll come over and we'll look for her together.'

He rings off, stands frowning at the phone.

'Who was that?'

'Bill Dunphy's wife. Their kid, Sally, hasn't come in from school.'

'You know Mrs Dunphy?'

'I do business with Bill. Elinor's worried. Naturally. They live just round the corner from the school and Sally always goes straight home.'

'Elinor?'

'Sally is Melissa's friend. Elinor thought she might be here.'

'Elinor Dunphy?'

'Sally's their only child. Elinor had several miscarriages before they got Sally. Something to do with her fallopian tubes.'

'Elinor's?'

'Bill wanted a big family. He blames her tubes.' He smiles, wryly. 'As if she needs a decoke.'

'You know Elinor Dunphy?'

'I've met her.'

'How many times?'

'Oh lord, how should I know?'

'Where?'

'At Bill's club—when I've picked Melissa up from school—in the supermarket.'

'You meet her in the supermarket?'

'I don't meet her, we run across each other.'

'What's she like?'

'Elinor?' He puts the name up between us, sounding casual. 'She's a nice woman.'

'Is she reasonable?'

That's a gibe against myself, my silly soft self that's still squirming. But he takes it another way. 'For God's sake!' He turns his back. 'I'm going to talk to Melissa.'

'What about?'

'Sally, of course. To find out if she knows anything.'

I go too. It's Sally Dunphy's mother who concerns me.

Melissa is watching an Australian soap opera on television. She looks up peakily. Arthur asks how she is feeling. I put my hand on her forehead. It is cool, and she made a good lunch.

Arthur asks about Sally. She hasn't come home from

school, has Melissa any idea where she might be? Melissa shakes her head. Arthur says does Sally talk to people? Would she, on her way to her house, be likely to stop and talk to someone? Melissa watches a man rope a steer. She perceptibly moves her head.

'Suppose,' says Arthur, sitting on his heels beside her, 'someone were to offer Sally sweets. Would she take them?' Melissa frowns, it is a tricky question. '*You* wouldn't!' cries Arthur. The man and steer go down in a cloud of dust. Melissa nods. Arthur reaches out and switches off the television. 'Listen to me, my girl, if I've told you once, I've told you a hundred times. You never speak to strangers in the street and you never ever accept anything from them. They may offer you sweets, dolls, trinkets—' his voice sharpens—'a ride in their car, on a donkey, on an elephant, no matter what—you must *never* go anywhere with anyone you don't know. Are you listening?'

Melissa touches her throat to remind us she is not well. Arthur has started to shout. I put my hand on his shoulder, tell her, gently, that we'd like to talk about Sally Dunphy. 'Your best friend. Did you see her this morning?' Melissa nods. 'Where?'

'In the playground.'

'What was she doing?'

'Playing.'

'Did she say anything about meeting anyone? Or going anywhere?' Melissa shakes her head, looks deep into the empty television screen. 'Sally hasn't come home from school. Her mother's worried. You know her mother. So does Daddy. You both know Elinor Dunphy.' They exchange looks. Behind Melissa's is coercion. I've seen her do it before. When she was a baby it was 'give me what I want or I'll hold my breath, go into convulsions and die'. Now it is for the television to be switched on— or else.

Arthur looks away. 'We're not getting anywhere.' He switches on the television.

The phone rings. I move to answer it but he is there first, picks up the receiver. 'Elinor? Thank God. I know,' he says. What does he know? 'I understand.' That's something, understanding is what we all want, me especially. There are two schools of thought here: he understands Elinor Dunphy because he doesn't know her enough, or because the more you know, the less you understand: or because he knows her in a way he has never known me, because he can penetrate her thoughts and he never gets past the skin of mine. 'I'm so glad!' He puts down the phone, turns to me. 'Sally's home. She lost her ballet shoes and stayed behind to look for them.'

'I bet it's put years on her.'

'On Sally?'

'On Elinor. It would on me.'

I can't believe in the word processor who's happy going upstairs with Arthur once a week while her father plays bowls. Please God no one's as reasonable as that.

Elinor Dunphy I believe in. I am calling on her, I am about to see her in the flesh. She must be wonderful in the flesh—tall, slender, talented, vibrant. I am never vibrant, I just get into a state.

She has bewitched my husband and my daughter. The witching of my husband I must accept, I could have accepted it of my son. But Melissa and I are playmates, I share her life—and we are going to share Elinor Dunphy.

She lives in a house which, though acquired from her husband, is wholly hers. It proclaims her: behold she wrought me, my paint is her choice, my curtains her making, my garden her planting, she allows my occasional weed, and my ground, if not sacred to her feet, is where she mostly treads. She chose me from a million desirable residences in this area which she has found desirable.

The walls of her house are faced with aggregate composed of millions of tiny flints, mostly ginger, with here and there one which is plum-coloured or a bit of mica which catches the sun. I've taken a couple of glasses of sherry to strengthen my nerve, but the grits dazzle me. There's nothing random about them, each is part of a mosaic protecting the brickwork. I couldn't put a pin between them—I have tried, with the pin belonging to the awful bunch of silk violets I have on my lapel.

I put the violets away in my handbag. I am starting to think—the sherry was another mistake—that Elinor Dunphy is a protected species.

I ring the bell and the daily help opens the door. I ask is Mrs Dunphy in and she says 'You're Mrs Appleton.' It's a shot to repel boarders.

'I'd like a word with her,' I say. The word is seductress, says it all, the theft of my husband and child, the discrediting of my life, and describes sinuous, snaky, successful Elinor Dunphy.

'Come in.' The home help turns her back, leaving me to follow. She's wearing an old-fashioned pinafore with muzzy roses all over it.

Elinor Dunphy has two husbands, hers and mine, two daughters, hers and mine, a lovely home with a double garage—she drives her own car—and this treasure she grapples to her with hoops of coffee and nearly new castoffs. She is definitely a protected species. I can't harm her but I can get her to do something for me, I can get her to give me a new image in place of the word processor.

'We won't talk on the step,' says the home help, and goes into a creative kitchen—handcrafted tiles, wall units finished in high-density laminate (I read the Wickes' booklets). 'I've just made coffee. Do you take sugar?' The muzzy roses and the lime-green fixtures give the place a cottagey feel.

'I really came to see Mrs Dunphy.'

'I'm Mrs Dunphy.'

This must be Elinor's mother I think—but no, she's not old enough. Her aunt then, or maybe an in-law, Bill Dunphy's brother's widow up from the country to shell the peas—there's a colander full of peas on the table.

'Mrs Elinor Dunphy,' I insist, politely.

'That's me.' She turns, and I get a proper look at her face—as seen in Tesco's and behind the wheel of Ford Escorts. It is a basic face, the kit without the identi. She has plentiful hair, wavy, though not natural and soon she'll have to tint. Her figure is quite meaty. She has capable hands and hockey calves. She says, 'I recognised you, I saw you once with Melissa.'

'What a pretty pinafore you're wearing.'

She looks at me askance. 'Do sit down. Milk in your coffee? Or cream?'

I could have kept the violets on, she has absolutely no style. I tell her I like her copper hood over the cooker. 'Sort of medieval, goes with belted earls and roast swan.' I am babbling.

'It's an extractor duct.'

She is busy with the percolator, I can see she's a dedicated house-woman. Nothing is allowed to retain its original state, certainly not the smells. She is here to transform the crudities of earth and air. Making a good life fulfils her. It's nice for her, it's nice for her family. But what of Arthur? Confused, I ask myself does he prefer a food- to a word-processor?

'I came to enquire after your little girl.'

'Sally?'

'Is she all right?'

'Quite, thank you.'

'I was worried. Such things happen.'

'That was kind of you.'

'Arthur was very concerned.'

'He is a caring man.'

The point at issue is what does he care about? She brings me coffee in a rustic mug. The coffee smells delicious, her husband comes down every morning to the best Colomban, freshly ground.

'I've already had mine.' She stands facing me across the peas, beautiful peas, green and glistening. She touches them with her finger, then takes the colander to the sink, a double unit, stainless steel, with mixer taps.

'I mustn't hinder you.'

'I take a break about this time and listen to "Morning Story".'

'You like listening to stories?'

'As a rule. Today's was too fanciful for my taste. It was about child abuse.'

'That's fanciful?'

'At coffee-time, yes. Don't you think so?' She smiles, picks out a yellow pea and throws it in the pedal-bin. She examines the rest, stirring them with her finger. 'I'm sorry I disturbed you last evening, I thought Melissa would know where Sally was. They're such friends.'

'So my son says. You know him, I think. You know Melissa, you know Arthur. I am the only one not in the know.'

'I hope we're rectifying that omission.'

'Call me Winnie.' She looks out of the corner of her eye, sizing me up, any moment now she will guess my weight. 'Arthur calls you Elinor. I daresay you often see him.' Once a week I daresay.

She inclines her head graciously, like the Queen Mum—in a pinafore. 'He comes to discuss business with my husband.'

'Rokeby's business?' I am putting two and two together to make a different four: no dad, no bowls, just husband Dunphy away in the office, Sally Dunphy in school, Elinor going upstairs with Arthur.

She runs cold water through the peas. It has been estimated that words account for only seven per cent of communication, the rest is achieved by movement and tone of voice. 'And Melissa comes to us for lunch.'

'Melissa has lunch at school.'

'Except when she comes here.'

'She always tells me about her school lunch, what she had, who she sat next to, who wouldn't eat the cauliflower cheese—'

'Little girls can be fanciful.' That word again, chosen this time to spare my feelings.

'Melissa is imaginative, she takes after me.'

She says firmly, 'Veracity does not come naturally to every child.'

'Are you worried about Sally?'

'Sally is thin-skinned, I would know at once if she was lying.'

'But could she be a whole hour looking for her ballet shoes?'

She smiles a handling smile, handling me. 'I shall speak to Melissa about coming here without your knowledge. It was wrong of her. I never hesitate to correct a child, even if it isn't mine.'

Motherhood, I'm told, is what my daughter admires in her. I don't believe it.

X

TOM THACKER LAUGHED when he saw her, absurdly thin, not delicate or pitiable, she put him in mind of a sparky insect. One of the workers and a survivor, definitely.

'Bet you can't do this.' On her toes she pirouetted, ballet style.

'I'd break my bloody neck if I tried.'

'It's easy getting up, it's how long you can stay up that counts.' She added, as to someone stating the obvious, 'Of course!' Unable to maintain balance in her canvas sneakers she tottered, swayed, and came down beating the air with her hands. She was cross, made herself no allowance for not having the proper shoes. 'Dammit, I can *dance* on my points.'

'What's the point?'

She frowned, she took him seriously, even his jokes, especially his jokes. 'It's ballet. You be the practice bar.' She leaned on him while she extended one leg horizontally behind her. She probably weighed about two and a half ounces, but her grip was firm.

On the bus she said 'I'd make an apple pie if I had any flour.'

'You'll manage.' He was trying to forestall a visit to the shops.

'You crazy? You can't make a pie without pastry and you can't make pastry without flour.'

Fortunately her attention was caught by the Christmas tree outside the Church of Christ, Scientist, and she was counting the gift-wrapped packages as they passed the stop for the shopping centre. Shopping with her was a hazard. Besides being short in stature, she was short-sighted and had to take each item off the shelf to examine it. She had been known to climb the shelves in order to reach things at the top. Store managers didn't like it.

'Your hair's too long. It's halfway down your bloody neck,' she said, and they both laughed.

When he had to face the store managers Tom found himself saying, 'She's good at climbing, she won't break anything.' He resented their attitude, he reminded them that she was showing an active interest in their wares. How many customers took the trouble to negotiate a wall of jam and marmalade to get to the treacle? He assured them that she was sure-footed and capable of picking her way between the Victoria sponges. He denied that she was undisciplined. Hers was a strict personal code.

When they got indoors she took off her coat, shook out the skirt of her dress. 'Like it?'

'I've seen you in it before.'

'It's Nina Ricci.'

'Very nice.'

'You want to be careful what you believe. People will tell you anything.'

'It's not Nina Ricci?'

'Does it look like it is?'

'On you, yes.'

She rolled up her sleeves, pushed a silver bangle over her elbow. 'What would you like for dinner?'

'I had dinner.'

'What did you have?'

'Pork chop, two veg. sultana pudding and custard.' He did not miss the constriction of her throat as she swallowed. 'What did you have?'

'A lovely bit of corned beef.'

'I thought they had stopped the free dinners.'

'If they did, I'd be starving, wouldn't I?'

Tom had heard that stomachs shrank in proportion to the amount of food put into them. Hers would always have been small, she was no more than a capsule of bone. But there was such a thing as too little of a little. 'There's a piece of pizza left from yesterday.'

'Junk food,' she said scornfully. 'You're going to have some good home cooking.'

'I was thinking of you.'

'You know I don't eat between meals.'

'What I know about you wouldn't cover a penny stamp. I have to surmise.'

'You do that.' She bustled away.

Tom's surmisals hadn't got him very far. Besides being in a cloud about her, he had found the cloud thickening about his own self. It was no use asking questions like why and what for. He had done so a few times and the answer had been to please her, which was only half an answer and made him a daddy figure.

He drank a whisky standing. He had no practical problems with himself, he was healthy, young, gainfully employed, had friends, and was thinking of marrying a girl called Kate Reed.

What had happened—call it a situation because of their placements in time and space in relation to each other—had been so swift and unlikely it confused him even to think about it. He couldn't remember how it had started: one minute she was walking on her hands in Goshawk Road, the next she was in his flat, rattling pans. No beginning, and he reckoned the end would come when it suited her chemistry. His own was acting irresponsibly.

She came in carrying a plate, treading carefully, thumbs over the rim, pleased, like one who sees her work turn out well.

'There,' she put it down on the table, 'get yourself round that.'

'What is it?'

'Shepherd's pie with tomatoes, onion and chopped parsley.'

'I've nothing to eat it with.'

'Fingers were before forks.' She fetched cutlery and a cruet from the sideboard. 'Let me see you enjoy it.'

'Oh I am.' He took up the knife and mimed cutting across the plate. 'This looks good—' plunging in the fork and lifting it to his mouth—'it *is* good. You're a great cook.'

'That's because I like cooking. I even like peeling the potatoes. It's real food, takeaways are muck.' She put her elbows on the table, stared at the plate. 'I don't want anything left.'

'I'm having trouble with my waistband.'

'I've done stewed fruit for after.'

'There,' he said, putting down his knife and fork. 'That was excellent.'

'You've left the gravy. I'll fetch you a spoon to finish it.'

He scraped about, the empty spoon tasted of metal. She went away and came back with a bowl. In it was a single dark green leaf.

'What's this?'

'I told you, stewed fruit.' She peered myopically at the leaf. 'Anyone can see it's rhubarb.'

'Rhubarb leaves are poisonous.'

'That's a nice thing to say! Think I'm trying to do you in?'

'Of course not. You won't mind if I just eat the fruit so as to be on the safe side?'

'You think my cooking's poison!' Her eyes swam behind her glasses.

'Don't be silly.'

'You do so!'

'Look, I'll eat the bloody leaf. OK?'

If ever anyone had told him he would do that to please her, he would have told them to go hang. As it was, the leaf tasted foul, he contrived to smuggle it into his handkerchief under cover of blowing his nose.

She said, 'Don't let's fight, I'm sick and tired of fights.' Looking at him through her pebble lenses she was a hundred years old.

He said, 'I never fight with the cook. And you're never tired.'

'It's them. I couldn't get to sleep last night.'

'What were they doing?'

'Grunting and snarling, I heard through the wall, like bears.'

'Bears?'

'Fighting!'

There was fear in her voice, some of what he felt for her was pity—and pity you had to beware of. 'One of these days they're going to want to know where you get to.'

'Not them, they don't care. I tell them I'm at my friend's house.'

'Suppose they find out?'

'It's none of their business.'

The way they treated her, it wasn't. Sometimes he had a thought that they were the sort of people who would make it their business. But it was all so innocent, and so funny, funny peculiar, funny comical and—yes—it was fun. How could he tell anyone about the fun? There was at least one person he should tell. He would, when the right moment came: 'Kate, you're not going to believe this . . .'

'Look,' he said, 'I'm going to get my hair cut. Why don't you lie down on the bed and rest?'

'You'll be back for tea!'

No question, just ferocity. Inside her beetle-case she was as fierce as a beetle.

'I'll be back before you know it.'

She went with him to the door, helped him on with his coat, brushed his shoulders. 'I've got a nice kipper for your tea.'

Kate walked along gazing at the houses in his street. They were old, what would be called lower middle class, cut up into flats. She noticed a plaster Alsatian in a window.

She knew most of what she needed to know about him, and the thought filled her with happy dread. Knowing your fate made you feel like that. But there were gaps in her knowledge, she hadn't met his parents or seen where he lived. 'Let me tidy up first,' he had said, and it endeared him because most men couldn't wait to get you into bed, made or unmade.

No. 31 was his, the windows full of lace net, the paintwork blistered, a folding pushchair in the porch. She rang the basement bell, touched her hair and the scarf at her neck, waited with a steadily quickening heartbeat.

A child opened the door—that was the first surprise—stretching up to reach the catch. She would be six or eight years old, wearing thick glasses which took up most of her face. She said 'Hi,' pushed the glasses higher on her nose.

'Is—does Mr Thacker live here?'

'Right.'

'Is he in?'

'Nope.'

There was a pause, the child seemed to think an end, and made to shut the door.

'When will he be in?'

'Who's asking?'

'Kate Reed. I work in the same office.' She added awkwardly, 'As him.' She felt at a disadvantage which, of course, she was. 'What's your name?'

'Rose-Marie.'

'Do you live here?'

The child nodded.

Another pause. A baby squalled somewhere inside the house. Kate felt a twinge of alarm. But told herself there could be several explanations: the child could live in another part of the house, or be visiting, or just difficult. 'Will he be long?'

'He's gone to get his hair cut.'

'Could I wait?'

'Suit yourself.'

Again she started to shut the door. Kate said quickly, 'It's awfully cold, would you mind if I waited inside?'

A stare of appraisal, Kate felt herself flushing. The child turned and went along a passage. The walls were painted dark green and chipped through to the plaster. Kate saw brown linoleum and a pram. God, please! she thought. The child—Marie yes, but she was no Rose—opened a door. Kate followed, her heart turning.

She saw at once that there was no one in the room. It was a bedsitter, with a cubbyhole filled with a cooker and a sink leading off. 'Small,' he had said, 'and I'm not tidy. I tend to dash out and leave everything.'

She could see he did, his shoes in a corner, his anorak over a chair, a daily paper gutted on the floor, dishes— though clean—on the table, and the divan-bed looking as if a restless animal had roughed it up.

'You can sit down.' The child pointed to a chair. 'I was going to tidy, I do it when he's not here, he doesn't like me fussing round him.' Kate perched on the edge of the chair, her handbag on her knee. 'I'd better get on with his tea, it's fried eggs and streaky.'

'You're going to cook?'

'If I know him he'll be looking for it directly he comes in. I suppose you could do with a cup?'

'Yes—if it's not too much trouble.'

'The kettle's on the boil. It won't take a minute.' It didn't. She went into the cubbyhole and came back immediately. 'I've put a nice piece of my gingerbread parkin in the saucer.' The saucer was empty, so was the cup. 'Drink up while it's hot, it'll warm you,' she said, serious, even kind.

Kate didn't know what to do. She sat holding the empty cup, feeling the biggest fool.

The child said proudly, 'He loves my parkin. I'm a great cook, he says.'

'Isn't there—is your mother here?'

The child's glasses blazed. 'What the hell's she got to do with it?'

Kate, taken aback, found herself apologising. 'I'm sorry—you said you live here—'

'So I do!'

'But who takes care of you?'

'I take care of him.'

'I mean when he's not here, when he's at work.'

'I do!' She stamped her foot, then as suddenly smiled, a smile of pure happiness, with only the slightest hint of victory. 'He takes care of me, we take care of each other.'

'That's nice. Tom's never said—' Kate's common sense came to her aid. Looking about, she saw signs of Tom's habitation, but not the child's. Surely there would be something—a doll, a picture-book, a hair ribbon, a packet of Smarties? 'Are you his sister?'

'No.'

'His cousin?'

'No.'

'You don't live here—'

'This is where we live.'

'It's Tom's flat, yes—'

'It's our house and that's our bed.' She pointed to the divan.

'Yours?'

'His and mine. Where we sleep.'

Kate tried, 'We used to play let's pretend when I was small—'

The glasses, which had blazed, magnified a couple of cold grey pebbles. 'Don't you know married people sleep together?'

*

Angie bites her biro. 'We shall want pictures.'

'Of me?'

'Naturally.'

'I don't look natural in a single exposure. I look arrested. It will take a whole reel to present me in the round.'

'We shall want you on the platform, telling your stories. When is your next engagement?'

'Tomorrow, in Middle Temple Hall.'

'Why there?'

'I'm going to tell a Gothic story.'

Angie frowns. 'What does your husband do?'

'Arthur? He prefers television, he never comes to my shows.'

'What I meant was what's his business. His job. We might mention it.'

'Oh I don't think you should. He's effluent controller at the sewage works.'

'Sewage?'

'Someone has to do it.'

'Doesn't it—' She looks round, her nose twitching. She has a spliced nose like a rabbit's.

'They have deodorant baths before they leave the plant. Like miners at the pit head. Of course there aren't so many effluent controllers. It's a pretty unusual job. You could say that Arthur and I are uniquitous.'

'Don't you mean unique?'

'I mean a combination of wickedness and difference.'

'I don't see you as wicked.'

'That's because of the method. I lead an ordinary housewife's life so that I can be wicked in my stories, so that I can do murder and it's legal and above board and no one can stop me. Being in touch, having people hang on my words, thousands of faces hung in the blackness of the auditorium, that's what I'm after. No bodies, I have had enough of bodies.'

I can say that because she doesn't know about Arthur and me, Arthur and the word processor. I don't want her to know, she might use it to round off *her* story—about a woman who mistrusts printed words whose husband betrays her with a woman who processes them. It would make a neat ending.

'Won't your stories go in one ear and out the other?'

'Oh no. The body evacuates, the brain retains.'

'But people forget.'

'I think everything you've ever experienced is stored away for future use and how it's used depends on you.'

'You use things you haven't experienced.'

'Experience is relative. I relate what I have had to what I haven't had. You could fill a whole issue of your magazine with me: romance, mystery, sport, sex, gardening, cookery, horoscopes, travel—I'd be in it all.'

'We only devote entire issues to royal weddings.'

'I could let you have the inside stories. Scandal, intrigue, heartache, dismay in high places. People love that sort of thing.'

'My editor wants a profile.' Angie puts down her biro with a grimace. She has bitten through to the ink. 'Don't you worry about losing your identity?'

'If I have an audience I'm saved.'

'You banish reality and manipulate people's minds!' At last she has found a crux for her article, her editor will call it thought-provoking.

'I manipulate people's minds—yes, we all do. It's what we're here for, it's become big business. But I don't mean to banish anything, least of all reality. What is reality?'

Before she can tell me, Arthur puts his head round the door and asks who am I talking to.

'Nobody.'

Arthur says, 'It's a bad habit.'

Hovis, our cat, stirs and wakes and sits blinking on the rush-bottomed chair. He is the death of Angie.